Caffeine N

Harder Than The Rest

Garry Bushell

With

Craig Brackenridge

Fiction aimed at the heart
and the head..

Published by Caffeine Nights Publishing 2021

Published in England by
Caffeine Nights Publishing
Amity House
71 Buckthorne Road
Minster on Sea
Isle of Sheppey
ME12 3RD

caffeinenights.com
caffeinenightsbooks.com

Printed in England by CMP (uk) Limited
Also available as an eBook

British Library Cataloguing in Publication Data
A CIP catalogue record for this book is available from the British Library

ISBN: 978-1-913200-18-3

Everything else by
Default, Luck and Accident

HARDER THAN THE REST
A Harry Tyler novel

By GARRY BUSHELL
WITH CRAIG BRACKENRIDGE

For my wife and family, I love you all.

And Terry, who was always there when it matters.

Acknowledgements

Garry Bushell would like to thank: Darren Laws and Caffeine Nights, the Bushwhacker, and too many good friends to mention – you know who you are. Thanks also to my old pals in the Cockney Rejects, Cock Sparrer and Iron Maiden who are nothing like the band depicted in this book whatsoever.

Craig Brackenridge: Cheers once more to Garry and Mr H for the Chislehurst connection. A big ye-haw to my jockabilly neighbours and many thanks for inspiration to all the great writers who worked on The Sweeney, Out, Fox, The Fear and The Squeeze. Dedicated (once again) to I, P, F and the beasts.

Chapter One

May 13, 1990. 5.30am

It was just after dawn on Hackney Marshes, one of the rare times that the common was deserted. A light mist stretched as far as the Cut, the scent of lilac and hawthorn blossom sweetened the air, and aside from the *"frarnk"* of a passing heron, the stillness was disturbed only by the crackle of police radios and hard men having harder conversations.

"Did you know him well, sir? Or is it best I don't ask?"

DCI Roy Pryor bit his lip and choked back a tear.

"Sir?" DI Stephen Pouncey, whose murder case this was, tried again.

Pryor turned away for a moment. Did he know him well? Better than well. He'd known his father; he'd watched him grow up. He had been at his passing out parade at Hendon. He'd been proud to see him transfer to the CID twenty-nine months later, and prouder still when he had joined his unit. He looked again at Mark Brennan's brutalised face and fought back a wave of nausea.

So many cuts, so much blood...

The face of the corpse had been slashed so deeply and viciously that his attacker could easily have been Freddy Krueger rather than a psychopathic East London thug, as was more likely. The crossed hammers carved into the centre of the victim's forehead were a bit of a clue.

"He's one of ours, Steve," he said finally. Then he corrected himself gruffly. "Was one of ours..."

The senior detective seemed to physically shrink as he spoke, as if some small part of him had also perished there in the lonely East End mud.

Royston Pryor had seen many gruesome murders over his long years of service. None had affected him quite like this. Mark Brennan had been one of the most promising undercover operators in the Met. He had a happy marriage, a great record and a glittering career ahead of him. Everything was going his way.

Until he had met the Bishops.

***

FOUR HOURS EARLIER

Ilford.

Woozy from sleep, the woman squinted through the peephole of her front door trying to work out who was repeatedly ringing her doorbell at such an ungodly hour. Her first thought was it would be her husband, but she didn't recognise the caller in the glare of the porch light at all. He was one of the ugliest men she had ever seen. His nose was large and squashed, as if someone had tried to hammer it flat with a mallet, and his heavy-lidded eyes looked distinctly lop-sided. She dropped her right hand to her belly and patted it, as if to reassure her unborn child that all was well.

Aware that he was being scrutinised, the man held a Metropolitan Police warrant card up to the spy-hole. Relieved, the woman undid the heavy stainless steel security chain and opened the door. She smiled but as she started to say "hello" the stranger shoved her violently back against the hall wall and stubbed out a cigarette on her forehead.

Before she could scream, he clasped a hand over her mouth, pushing hard, and then pulled it back and knocked her out with a straight left to the jaw.

She only caught a glimpse of the burly men in balaclavas who followed in his wake, and a lingering smell of diesel.

The nightmare was just beginning.

Chapter Two

TWO YEARS EARLIER

Monday, July 11, 1988. Wolverhampton.
The man in the black, battered Bell Bullitt motorbike helmet and matching leather jacket watched the second hand on his Rolex Cellini.
Soon. Very soon.
He squeezed the Colt 1911 in his shoulder holster through the leather absent-mindedly, as if to make sure the gun was still there. 9.34pm became 9.35pm. Finally. He nodded slightly. "Now," he muttered. He squeezed the clutch of the Norton Commando as a second man dressed in exactly the same plain, anonymous style jumped on behind to ride pillion. Then he cranked her up.
VROOOM!
It took four minutes eleven seconds to reach the jewellery shop in Cleveland Street. He parked up just as the stolen Range Rover smashed straight through the front of the jewellery shop. The bikers dismounted and ran full-tilt to the car. They took sledgehammers out of the boot and began smashing display cases, while the Range Rover driver and his passenger collected the hard stuff and the Tom in a large canvas bag.
They were in and out in under ninety seconds. Two minutes sixteen seconds later both vehicles were abandoned and the four men were on their way back in a freshly acquired Ford Fiesta that had been parked in a nearby street an hour before. It was only then that they heard the first police siren fading into the distance as they sped away in the opposite direction.
At 9.47pm, with jacket, helmet and the semi-automatic deposited in the waiting black sack, Terry Bishop checked his

Rolex again, nodded and walked into the wings as Butch "Halfwit" Halfin's drawn-out drum solo at the end of 'Profession of Violence' built to its closing crescendo. He took the Fender Strat from Mikey, his guitar tech, sauntered on stage and launched straight into the soaring opening riff of Iron Hammer. The rhythm section joined after four bars and then Wolf Bishop cart-wheeled in from stage right, grabbing his mic just in time for the first verse: *"We're Iron Hammer, we're out tonight/Iron Hammer, we live to fight/We don't give a fuck/So you're out of luck/We're Iron Hammer, we're out tonight."*

His voice was a tough growl, nearer to punk than metal but melodic enough to appeal to both camps. The 1100 capacity crowd at Wulfrun Hall were going seriously mental, thrashing their heads about and punching the air. Clenched fists and devil signs abounded. There didn't seem to be a single punter who wasn't singing along: *"Straight from the streets, where no one cares/Broken bottles and concrete stairs/You'd love us gone but we're still here/A movement, an army... and we want our share.*

Cos we're Iron Hammer, we're out tonight/Iron Hammer, we live to fight/We don't give a fuck/So you're out of luck/We're Iron Hammer, we're out tonight."

Naturally the "fucks" were loudest, shouted with gusto and punctuated by more clenched fists than a Communist Party rally. Not that the crowd or the band were that way inclined.

'Iron Hammer' wasn't the group's biggest selling song. But it was the stand-out track from their DIY debut EP, the one that announced their arrival to the jaded rock world. For their hardcore fans it was the must-hear anthem. Like 'Ace of Spades' for Motorhead, 'Anarchy In The UK' for the Sex Pistols or 'The Trooper' for Iron Maiden. It was also their shortest song at 2.31. That gave them ample time to leave the stage and return triumphantly for the set-closer, 'Fort Vallance' – their first Top Ten hit – bringing with it the traditional stage invasion of their "Iron Army", heavily inked thugs many of whom had followed "the Hammer" since their earliest gigs at the Ruskin Arms in East Ham, the Bridge House in Canning Town and the ultra-violent, god-forsaken Tidal Basin which was somewhere south of Hell.

At some venues, the security staff had naively tried to prevent the Iron Army from accessing the stage. It was not a mistake they would ever make twice.

***

By the time the set had finished at 10pm, a hold-all containing forty-seven rings, some silver novelty gifts and eighteen three-piece necklace and earring sets was already on its way back to East London in an old Grenada driven slowly but steadily by road manager Vic Galanis. The haul, mostly 22ct gold and gems, was worth around £37K. Not bad for three minutes' graft.

Normally the stash would have been packed into a concealed strongbox built into the false wall of the merchandise truck, but Terry had a buyer over from Amsterdam who wanted to seal the deal and be on his way home. Sweet as...

***

Terry Bishop was just drying himself after a shower when he heard a light knock on his dressing room door. He opened it slightly to see the bright blue eyes of Sylvie Forester, a young, cute and pleasantly curvy rock writer from *Kerrang!* magazine with a mess of auburn hair. "You were amazing," she gasped as she glimpsed his face. She had the smile of a religious convert.

"Come in, Sylv."

His voice was low and gravelly with more than a hint of sandpaper, she thought. He held the door open for her and caught a strong whiff of Estelle Lauder's 'Beautiful'. In this particular case, Estelle wasn't wrong. The young self-proclaimed "24-hour party animal" was a stunner.

"Seriously," she continued, "that was one of the greatest shows I have ever...oh..."

Terry smiled inwardly. She'd clocked the cock.

"Sorry, Sylv, I was just getting changed."

"No, no. My fault for just barging in."

He picked up a towel and wrapped it around the source of her embarrassment.

"Fancy some toot?"

His grin could disarm a platoon of Paras. "Yeah...uh, yes please," she stuttered, grateful for the distraction.

Terry reached for his wallet and casually tipped about three grams worth of cocaine onto the copy of *Connoisseur* magazine on the table, chopping it quickly into fat lines with a gold Amex card.

"'Ere y'are." The words were rasped, not spoken.

He gave her a purpose-made glass sniff tube and she hoovered up about half a gram's worth greedily. As she passed the tube back, he held her wrist and looked into those sparkling baby blues. She was so young, he thought, so naive, so trusting. A proper fan girl, and consequently as objective as the Stasi.

"Please don't take this the wrong way, Sylvie, but you are such a beautiful woman. I..."

He didn't get to finish the sentence because she was on him like a dog on barbecue spill. If he'd had the Rolex on, he would have noted that they had gone from the knock on the door to his knob in her gob in little over four minutes.

It wasn't the best blow job he'd had that year, or even that week, but it was certainly the most enthusiastic.

As he slipped on a CP Company sweat top afterwards, Terry cynically calculated that that experience alone was good for a praise-packed feature in the next issue of Britain's biggest selling rock magazine and, if he played his cards right, a five-star review for the live double album that they were planning to release the following summer. So he was particularly gentle when he steered Sylvie out of the room and into One-Gin Denny's hands and asked him to drive her back to the Britannia.

"One-Gin will let you wait in my suite. Help yourself to room service."

"Oh, okay."

The disappointment in her voice clanged like a dropped cymbal.

"You don't mind, do you?" – his tone was concerned, almost pleading – "Only we have this post-gig band conference thing now and it might drag on. Proper pain in the arse, but we always have it after the opening night of a tour. You make yourself comfortable and I'll be straight back...for the...interview."

He winked and she melted.

"I'll get the recorder set up ready."

May 15, 1990. 9am.

The small group of pickets outside St George's College watched suspiciously as the jet black XJ-S with matching windows purred to a stop a few feet away from them. The women, all cleaners, had staged a wildcat strike after the building had been found to be riddled with deadly asbestos. So far their action was unofficial.

The Jag's driver, One-Gin Denny, stepped out of the gleaming vehicle and opened the back, kerbside door with a theatrical flourish. Vicky, the youngest of the pickets gasped as rock star Terry Bishop bowled out, with his brown eyes twinkling. His grin was as wide as Canning Town flyover. His sterner-looking brother Wolf emerged from the left-side door. One-Gin opened the boot and the three men carried boxes over to the picket line. One was stacked up with freshly bought breakfast food – sausage sandwiches, bacon rolls and so on –

along with teas and coffees; another contained basic shopping, enhanced with two magnum bottles of Moët. The last was full of cash stained with sweat from the Iron Hammer merch stall.

The women posed happily with the leather-jacketed local heroes as a photographer from the *Daily Mirror* took pictures. The rockers adapted their traditional pose – legs apart, thumbs in the bullet belt; Terry still smiling, Wolf, always the poseur, sucking in his cheeks to look more chiselled. In contrast to his brother's dark flowing locks, his black hair was cropped in a convict cut.

Even the older women flirted with "the boys", squeezing their arses like they were testing supermarket fruit and making suggestive remarks.

"You going to do a benefit for us Tel?" asked elderly Vi.

"He could give me the benefit any time," said Anne, almost drooling.

"Now, now, you know I'm with Sylv..."

"I won't tell 'er if you don't luv!"

"You need to start auditioning for wife number three," said Kathy, the youngest picket, who blushed at her own boldness.

"Leave it out darling, I'm still shelling out for the first one," Terry replied with a heart-felt chuckle.

They kidded around for about ten minutes. At some point, as hugs and kisses were exchanged, Kathy managed to slip her phone number into Terry's pocket.

"Power to the people!" he shouted at the snapper as he turned to leave.

"Solidarity!" added Wolf, punching the air with a clenched left fist.

And then they were gone.

***

Night didn't fall on Canning Town. It oozed up from the sewers and congealed. In the deepening shadows, just down from the Durham Arms, three Newham CID detectives were parked in an old, beaten-up Granada waiting for the deal; waiting to pounce. Their intel was good. A major cocaine deal was going down at 10pm in nearby Bidder Street. The officers were all as tough as stewing steak; all of them were armed.

The eldest, DS Dan Roberts, known uncharitably as Fat Dan, cleared his throat.

"Anyone got an oily?"

"Given up," grunted the driver, DC Tony Durrant.

"Never started," said DC Nick Wells.

"Thanks girls. Where's Wilson when you need him? He's always got fags."

"Yeah, where is 'e, Nick?"

"Called in sick...got this nasty rash come up on his back...quite wide too...a big old yellow streak..."

Wells let the words hang and then added softly, "This shouldn't be us."

"This is mine!" Roberts snapped. "We have been after these cow-sons for too long to stand aside and let any other goal-hanging buggers half-inch all the glory for taking them down."

He looked ahead glumly and drummed his fingers on the dashboard.

"How long we got?"

"Forty-five minutes until their meet time."

"I'll nip to the pub, buy a packet."

"Fuck off Dan. They'll clock you straight away. It's full of wrong'uns."

"So I'll jog on down to the Ordinance. I'll be back in five."

The DS got out of the Fiesta and walked off.

"Grumpy fat bastard. He's not smoking in this car."

19

"Back in five...a Jacks says he won't be back in under twenty minutes."

"Course he won't. He'll be in the boozer, he'll neck a crafty brandy or two."

"Eye up the barmaid – pointlessly – sling a cockle in the fruit machine...probably stop for a pie."

"Or three. Imagine if he actually tried jogging back. At the weight he is now, he's a heart attack waiting to happen...that's assuming he's actually got one to begin with."

"Ha. Yeah. But to hear him he talk, he could have been up there with McAvennie."

"Ah, Frank and Tony Cottee...what a double act."

"Dream team, mate. Red hot in '86. Mind you Frank scored even more off the pitch...Jenny fucking Blythe!"

He whistled. The detectives caught each other's eyes and laughed. It was the last thing they ever did.

Chapter Three

May 16, 1990. Limehouse.

Booty's Riverside Bar was so quiet it was like walking into a portrait, thought DCI Roy Pryor. There was no one behind the jump and just one figure at the far end of the Narrow Street boozer, motionless with her back to him staring out over the Thames which was shimmering in the summer heat. The back belonged to DI Shirley Kelly, one of the few detectives at Stratford nick who Pryor knew was as straight as a guardsman's back.

"Penny for them Shirl."

"They're all bad, guv."

Roy held out his hand to shake hers and she kissed his cheek instead.

"This is informal, right?"

"It has to be...the way things are. Sorry to hear about your guys."

"Sorry to hear about Mark Brennan."

"He was a good kid."

"How do you think he was rumbled?"

"He wasn't. He was grassed. Mark was too good to have been rumbled."

"Yeah. And I'd lay good odds that Nick Wells and Tony Durrant were set up too. They were in an unmarked car, both in civvies, and someone lobbed a petrol bomb underneath it."

"Someone?"

"A young kid on a BSA Panther, twelve maybe thirteen, is what DS Roberts saw."

"Why was Roberts out of the car?"

"Buying fags. They had a bit of time before the drug deal was due to go down. If it was ever actually happening. If my theory is correct, the snout was fed false intel."

"Is the snout talking?"

"He's done a Lord Lucan. Missing believed to be in Northern Cyprus."

"And Roberts?"

"DS Roberts seems genuinely gutted."

"Anything else?"

"There was a fourth officer, DC Wilson, Tony Wilson, who should have been there but rang in sick."

"So, four became two..."

Pryor sighed. "And the deal definitely involved the Bishop gang?"

"It involved the brothers themselves, according to Roberts. That was the intel. Presumably because of the quality and quantity of the cocaine being traded. But every investigation into the Bishops falls apart."

"Definitely a rotten apple."

"No, Roy. We'd sniff out one rotten apple. What we have here is a barrel load. It's like Stoke Newington was and Canning

Town is. Corkscrew bent. I'd say at least half of them are on the take."

"So what we do next cannot involve any local officers."

"Absolutely not. They can't get a sniff. We need to set up an operation that bypasses Stratford completely."

Pryor looked Kelly in the eye. "We'll need a proper briefing from someone with local knowledge."

"Count me in."

"There's something else."

"Go on."

"On the morning Mark was murdered, a group of masked men forced entry into a house and brutally abused a pregnant school teacher called Catherine O'Mara in every manner you can imagine."

"Dear God."

"She was five months pregnant, Shirley, and not long married."

"Christ."

"At the time we had no reason to think that the assault was anything to do with Mark's killing, but now we know that he and Sandra, his wife, had lived in that house until three weeks before it happened, so it seems extremely likely that the despicable attack on Catherine O'Mara was connected to Mark Brennan's murder. Catherine lost the baby. She's still in hospital."

"Have you seen her?"

"Yes. She's in a coma."

"It's a wicked world."

"And it's getting worse."

***

DCI Roy Pryor and DI Shirley Kelly were sitting in a soulless conference room at New Scotland Yard along with officers from technical support and DCI Colin McFaul from Covert Operations, accompanied by an up-and-coming DS Edward Richardson, who was widely known as "Rottweiler". Dark blinds covered every window.

McFaul convened the meeting, stating that he was acting on behalf of the Commissioner. Pryor introduced Shirley Kelly who gave a short but precise account of the Bishops' rise, using a projector and some hastily assembled slides. One graphic showed the correlation between a string of nationwide robberies and their 1988 UK tour.

"How did nobody notice?" asked Roy.

"Well it was noticed," she said. "But only afterwards..."

"So why not wait for their next show and catch them in the act?"

"Because the band were on stage when the robberies were committed."

"On stage? So how...", said McFaul.

"Roadies? The Iron Army?" added Pryor.

"The who?"

"Their entourage, sir. The investigating officers dismissed those possibilities. Eye witness descriptions of the robbers didn't fit the roadies at all. But they did fit the brothers, height, build etc, exactly. It was a mystery until one of the band's former road crew explained how it was done to reduce his sentence for an unrelated offence."

"Go on."

"It was quite ingenious. Iron Hammer had added a lengthy progressive rock anthem to their live set with extended drum and keyboard solos which dragged on for around thirteen minutes, long enough for the Bishops to leave the venue, commit the high-speed robberies, and get back before anybody in the audience noticed. Lighting effects added to the confusion, with the spotlight flipping between the synthesiser and the drums. Body doubles for Wolf and Terry – the guitar tech and one of the drivers – stood in the shadows, in sight but never fully seen. Standard magicians' misdirection. Apparently, there is a section in the song where the keyboardist throws machetes into the synthesiser."

"Very Keith Emerson," grunted McFaul. "And yes, it's all very ingenious. But again, why didn't we nick them on the next tour?"

"They moved on," Roy said glumly.

"Yes," said Shirley. "The road crew still deal in drugs and gross porn videos, but as far as we can tell the robberies stopped after that '88 tour."

"What's the source of the drug supply?" asked Mark Nixson.

"Family connections in Holland and Spain. Comes in containers, via Tilbury Docks."

"How gross is the porn?"

Shirley pulled a face. "Anal mostly. Illegal, but a small stretch."

She meant prison sentence but everyone present resisted cracking the obvious joke.

"What happened to the stolen jewellery?"

"Shifted quickly. Usually through Rathbone Street Market in Canning Town or through a bent jeweller over in Ingatestone with so-called celebrity clientele, footballers, boxers, Page 3 girls... you know the sort, the standard Athena Apollo mix. It's the Bishops' usual haunt."

Roy Pryor nodded. The Apollo, in Stratford, was a magnet for famous faces – and infamous ones. It was run by two brothers Pannychis and Christos Adamos, known as Panny and Chris, who didn't seem to mind their clientele's backgrounds as long as they were holding folding. You could see as many duckers and divers there as you could glamour models and soap actresses; and many an out-and-out villain too.

"The Bishops have fingers in enough pubs and clubs to wash the drug money," Shirley continued. "They also supply protection, own a luxury minicab firm and run prostitutes. Terry is into buying up property now. They're big, they're smart, their accountant is based in Jersey and they're growing closer to respectability by the week."

"Do they have any known connections to organised crime?" growled Rottweiler Richardson.

"The Knights."

"Jesus. Really?"

"Yeah," said Roy Pryor. "They're related to them through their mother, which explains why they're on friendly terms with Canning Town and Islington. They don't tread on each other's toes."

"Steven Knight is Terry Bishop's godfather," added Shirley Kelly – a revelation that was met with thoughtful silence.

"What about the rest of the band? What's the set-up there?"

"There's Sid Silverton on rhythm guitar, real name Derek, Julian 'Butch' Halfin also known as Halfwit on drums and Francis Bydewell, known as Frarnie, on keyboards," said Shirley. "As far we know they're not involved in the criminal side. They are jobbing musicians, plain and simple."

"And no criminal records?"

"None of them. Even the Bishops were only ever collared for minor offences in their teens. The usual stuff. Football disorders – generally West Ham away – and petty theft. But nothing for years because whenever we get close to a collar, the evidence goes missing. Files get mysteriously lost or the brothers appear to have been tipped off and change their plans. Their top 'soldier' is Donald Warwick, known as 'Mungo' who we believe strangled a young woman called Suzanne Summerville to death with her own tights in Plaistow Park two years ago. We had an eye witness prepared to testify but he had an unexplained change of heart. He packed in his job as a gas fitter and emigrated to New Zealand before the case came to trial. He told neighbours that he'd had a big win on the horses. We suspect his identity had been leaked to the Bishops."

Roy nodded. "We have good reason to believe Newham Crime Squad is hopelessly compromised," he said.

"Hence Operation Panther," said Colin McFaul.

"Yes."

Richardson growled. McFaul looked grim. "So, what's the plan, Roy?"

"I believe the best bet is we run an operation that none of the local boys know anything about. We'll need to send in another u/c. They won't be expecting that."

"He'll need brass balls after what happened to Brennan."

"Yes, he will. Mark, where's Harry?"

***

May 18, 1990. Oxfordshire.

A gleaming white Transit van with Deepdale Pharmaceuticals emblazoned proudly across its sides pulled up to the Benston Institute security gate. Reg Barone, the ferret-eyed security guard, stepped out of his gatehouse and lumbered over to the driver's window. For a man who had been expelled from the Met five years before for "conduct unbecoming", he had an exaggerated sense of self-importance. Barone was two stone overweight and seven lbs of that was unjustified arrogance. He did a double take when he noticed the driver. She was a model-level gorgeous with finely chiselled features, long blonde hair, distinctive sky-blue eyes and a smile so bright it could dazzle an Osmond. Her uniform – crisp white shirt, green tie and green v-neck jumper – looked a little on the large side, but it couldn't quite disguise the generous swell of her breasts. Even with unkempt hair and little make-up, she was clearly a knockout.

Barone regained his composure.

"Where's Steve today then?"

"He had to have a day off, something to do with his daughter." Her voice was soft, Reg thought. Surrey. Walton end. Too posh for van driving. "Nothing serious but it had to be dealt with. I'm the new cover for Saturday nights and all the other crap shifts."

He grunted. She flashed him a smile that could have melted a cheese sandwich at fifteen paces.

"You don't mind dealing with me today do you?"

"Not if you've got the correct paperwork."

What a charmer. She nodded and handed a delivery note to him, trying not to stare too hard at his nose which was red tinged with hints of green, like an unripe tomato. There was, she noticed, a remnant of breakfast bacon clinging to his teeth. His arteries must be more furred up than an Antarctic expedition.

Barone poured over the slip of paper as if it were the Nicene Creed; slowly checking each and every word.

"It says here Steven Richards as driver. Don't you have a delivery note with your own name on it?"

"Oh those silly berks at dispatch! They printed off the amended delivery note but they must have still given me the original. Honestly, if they spent more time focusing on the job and less time ogling my Charlies we'd have a lot less cock-ups."

Ogling her Charlies would have the opposite effect on me, thought Reg.

"They're always at it! It's as if they still haven't grasped the concept of a woman driver...like cavemen struggling to comprehend fire."

She leaned forward slightly; her breasts gained more definition as the green wool tightened around them. Barone's blotchy face reddened. He spluttered quietly and forced his attention back to business.

"And your name?"

"Victoria. Victoria Boosler. Vicky."

"Oh well...no harm done...Vicky. Just make sure it's all in order next time."

"I will..." she studied his name badge. "...Reginald."

For the first time that day he smiled.

"I'll open the gate. Take the first left before the main building and follow that round to 'goods in'. There'll be someone there to meet you but you might have to wait a bit for him seeing as it's the weekend and we're short-staffed. Be careful with him, he's a grumpy bastard."

Vicky Boosler suppressed the desire to laugh.

The heavy, ornate metal gates creaked apart slowly as the hydraulic system kicked into action. Vicky waited until they opened wide enough for the van then flashed him another big broad smile. "Cheerio! Hope you have a good weekend once your shift has finished."

Reg smiled back and gave her the thumbs up. Tricky Vicky could come again, he thought. Any way she wanted.

The Benston Institute was located in an old but well-maintained stately home. It sat in a small dip in the Vale of White House, on the far edge of North Wessex Downs, that made it almost invisible from the roads surrounding it. An ancient arboretum stretched along one side of the building offering further protection from curious ramblers and other prying eyes.

Discretion was required at the Benston, a world-class research facility which utilised animals in the pursuit of science. The words 'animal testing' did not appear anywhere on its website, but experiments were conducted routinely on small mammals, mostly rodents. The institute had a small incinerator room in what looked like a stable block near the back of the building where the stunned 'participants' quietly disappeared in a puff of smoke when their usefulness had come to an end.

The grand exterior of the building housed a state-of-the-art laboratory complex that was positively bursting with the latest scientific equipment in each hermetically sealed room. It was not a large concern, with only four main labs and a cluster of office space, but it was close enough to Oxford and the A40 to attract a small band of genius-level boffins who desired privacy and were not squeamish about vivisection.

Weekends at the Benston were usually quiet, and today was no exception. As the Deepdale van cruised slowly up the long drive, Victoria noticed that there were only two cars parked at the side of the main house. She pulled up to the metal shutter of the goods inward entrance and squirmed slightly in her seat as the door's machinery started up with a clatter and the shutter began to creep upwards. When it had cleared the height of the van, a second security guard appeared inside and motioned for her to pull forward into a concrete loading bay area. She smiled to herself as she noticed how much he looked like a heavier version of old Reg Barone at the front gate. They could almost have been twins. Where did they get these guys? Fat Old Fascist Bastards R Us? Or did they just fall face-first out of the ugly tree hitting every lateral branch on the way down? If there wasn't a security agency that specialised in hiring out cantankerous old codgers with thick moustaches, red noses and treble chins then maybe she should think about starting one.

South Africans, Jocks and Northerners were probably the grumpiest. Reg 2 looked even more miserable than Reg 1. What a fucking loser. If it rained soup he'd be out there with a fork and not a spoon.

Vicky slipped the van into first gear and rolled forward, stopping before the back of the vehicle was completely clear of the door. As she turned off the engine and started to open her door, Reg 2 sighed theatrically and motioned to her to move forward. She flashed her warmest smile at him and shrugged her shoulders, but this chap was made of stronger stuff.

"Move your vehicle forward," he yelled. "We can't accept deliveries unless the vehicle is fully within the building."

Reg 1 was right. They were Tweedle-Grump and Tweedle-Grumpier.

Victoria smiled again then leant forward as if she was scrabbling around for her keys. She was still fumbling when the guard lost patience and strode over to the driver's door to give her a piece of his mind. Woman drivers! He'd let her have it.

As he opened his mouth to shout, Vicky threw the door open with her full strength. The unexpected impact caught the guard off balance and sent him crashing to the ground clutching his chest in pain. "Now!" yelled Vicky. The back doors of the van swung open and three young men leapt out. Reg 2 was on his hands and knees struggling to his feet when a Doctor Marten boot swung at his jaw and connected fully. Lights out.

Deepdale driver Steve Richards had not been absent from work that Saturday at all. There had been no family matter that required his attention. He had turned up promptly at Deepdale's warehouse in High Wycombe and made his way up the M40 to the Institute with little more than a pallet of stock. It should have been an easy day and all on time and a half. Drop the delivery, maybe have a bit of chat and a cuppa with the Benston security lads, then back down with the van then straight over to Adams Park to see his beloved Wycombe Wanderers kick off at 3pm. He had almost reached his destination when he was forced to grind to a halt. Ahead, an old Renault with its bonnet raised was blocking both sides of the country lane. The alarm bells should have been ringing but a slender young woman with long, brown hair was standing close by and the look of relief on her face when she saw him made him pull over rather than slamming into reverse. Steve stepped from the van and asked her if she was okay. He did not hear the young man who crept up behind him, nor the swing of the cosh that struck him hard on the side of his head, although he later recalled an unexpected smell of body odour and curry.

When he came around fifteen minutes later Steve found himself stripped down to his underwear, bound, gagged and lying on the wet grass behind some bushes.

***

Three young men and a girl, all wearing balaclavas, stood over the Benston guard as he tried to get off the cold, concrete floor of the loading bay.

"Easy tiger," hissed Tim Robb menacingly as he pressed his boot down on the guard's windpipe. Tim was a handsome, broad-shouldered young man and beneath his balaclava was a mane of tousled, curly hair. His army greens and camouflage jacket gave him the look of a weekend warrior, but his face was etched with twenty-five years of wealth and public school entitlement – the stench of upper middle class privilege stuck to him like a cold sweat.

Victoria Boosler stared down at Reg 2 as he groaned on the ground and loosened her Deepdale Pharmaceuticals tie. Beside her was Tim's elder brother Jake, a towering streak of piss who never seemed to wash and whose bushy beard always smelt like left-over lentil dhal. Next to him was new recruit Pete Harrison. Both men carried baseball bats.

Tim pulled the security guard to his feet and gave him a sharp dig in the back with the tip of a crowbar. The guard gasped in pain then felt the hair at the back of his head being gripped tightly.

"Now don't fuck us about," Tim hissed in the man's ear. "We know there's only you and that fucking butcher Mendelssohn here today, so take us straight to him or god help me I will knock every single yellowing tooth out of your sorry plebeian head."

"Who are you?" Reg 2 croaked.

"SAC, darling," said Victoria.

"SA...C?"

"As in Sack Animal Cruelty. You vermin have been getting away with murder for too long."

"What do you want?"

"For fuck's sake, this isn't the fucking Wogan Show," snapped Tim. "This isn't a discussion, chum. Take us to Mendelssohn or my colleagues here will introduce you to the business end of their baseball bats. It's your decision but make it quick."

The guard grunted something that sounded like an agreement and Tim pushed him towards the locked door that led into the main building.

As he fumbled for his keys, Jake took a careful look out of the main entrance and scanned the grounds for any movement, but the only action was a passing swallowtail – *Papilio machaon*, he noted – and a soft wind rustling the distant trees. It was as if Mother Earth were nodding in conspiratorial approval of their actions. You couldn't hear the cars zooming past on the A40, or the anguished cries of the captive creatures inside. It was their sworn mission in life to stop one and liberate the others.

***

Harvey Mendelssohn had come into work that morning to finish off a presentation for the board, or so the good doctor had told his wife. In truth his motivation for this dedication was as much to escape from the formidable Khristyana as it was to dot the i's and cross the t's of his latest work on the use of mouse protein to treat breast cancer. His mood had improved as soon as he started the ignition and continued to do so as he drove at a leisurely pace through the beautiful Oxfordshire countryside. Sometimes coming to work was the only relaxing part of the day as his wife, who in many ways resembled the Battleship Potemkin in a twin set, ran their social life like a presidential campaign. Some evenings he barely made it through the front door before being ordered out into the night to attend some hellish charity function, dull house party, or bore-stuffed gala dinner. There wasn't a parents committee at their children's schools that she hadn't been involved in.

The Institute had its moments of frenzied activity, but they were few and far between. Generally the scientists were left to their own devices as long as they maintained a certain tally of small advances peppered with the occasional breakthrough discovery to keep the board happy.

Harvey sincerely believed that their research had to be done for the greater good, whether that be creating a life-saving medicine or a shampoo that did not torture the eyes. The benefits for human health far outweighed any discomfort or passing pain suffered by rats, mice and rabbits. There was no alternative. The generous wages paid by the Benston Institute were only a small part of what had brought him there. Science and the advancement of humanity were what drove him.

BBC Radio 3 parped gently from a small transistor set on top of a filing cabinet – the not-long deceased Herbert von Karajan's masterly performance of Brahms's 'A German Requiem'. Mendelssohn was aware of Benjamin Britten's view that using classical music as a background accompaniment to daily tasks was "a devaluation of the currency of sublime art", but he found Brahms both soothing and conducive to thought. He settled down to peruse some paperwork and sip his freshly brewed loose leaf Puerh tea. By chance he caught his face looking back at him from the speculum on his desk. Not a pretty sight. It was an aging visage; saggy, increasingly red and thickened from his claret consumption. He studied the tiny veins around his nose in the reflection. He would probably have to cut back, but Chateau Grand Moulin Macquin was one of the few things that made home life sufferable.

Ker-blam! The moment of quiet reflection tempered with self-loathing was shattered by a boot loudly kicking open his office door. Four masked louts burst in with a bloodied security guard who they forced roughly onto the floor in front of him.

What? Who? How? Why?

Tim Robb took three lunging steps and heaved the baffled boffin out of his chair, hurling him to the ground alongside the groaning guard. The steel toe of Robb's boot crashed hard and deep into Mendelssohn's flabby guts, and the scientist gave a gasp that sounded like his last breath.

"Where's the door pass to lab four?" Robb yelled.

"There...there's nothing in there at the moment."

"Liar! Do you think we haven't done our homework? Who the fuck do you think you're dealing with?"

Mendelssohn groaned in pain but said nothing. He tried to control his breathing and commit every moment of this fresh hell to memory.

The shouty man was clearly in charge and, despite his yobbish manner, plainly middle class – a radical lecturer perhaps, or a mature student, if that wasn't an oxymoron. He had a wild flicker in his eyes that could either indicate sadism or manic depression. Possibly both. The others...

Tim glanced at the desk and noticed the tea. Still gripping Mendelssohn tightly around the throat, he reached out with his other hand and grabbed the cup and hurled the hot contents of the Yunnan Province's finest straight into his victim's face. Mendelssohn yelped in pain. Tim then smashed the cup on the hard parquet wood floor leaving just the handle with a jagged splinter of ceramic attached in his hand. He used this to cut a slice across Mendelssohn's right cheek. The scientist let out a high-pitched sound that was half a scream and half an agonised groan.

"That's enough," Pete Harrison spoke for the first time.

Tim turned and looked directly into Pete's eyes.

"You wanted in?" he yelled. "Well you're fucking in now, so mind your own business and watch that fucking door."

White specks of spittle were shooting from his mouth as he tightened his grip on the scientist's neck and rifled through his pockets. He looked deranged.

"Don't make this scumbag scientist a martyr," Pete said evenly. "That would backfire on us; tar us all as lunatics, terrorists and murderers. It would play into their hands. We're liberators, we're making our point. If you kill him, our message gets drowned out by political propaganda with a large side order of hate heaped on hysterically by the fuckin' Tory press."

Tim hesitated.

"He's right," said Victoria from the corner of the room; Jake nodded vaguely in agreement too. "We're not the oppressors, they are." She waved her finger in a wide arc from the scientist to poor old Reg 2 who now looked close to lifeless. "Let's do what we came here to do and get out."

Tim grunted. He pulled a security pass from Mendelssohn's trouser pocket and held it aloft with a flourish; then he moved away from the scientist/torturer slowly, his gaze flitting between Pete and Victoria.

"Okay. Leave these fucking parasites here and get ready. I don't want a single thing in this slaughterhouse left in one piece."

Tim shouldered Pete out the way and headed down the hallway to the lab. His team followed behind dutifully even though the vicious beating of the scientist had taken the edge off Liberation Day. Not that it stopped Pete breaking expensive lab equipment as gleefully as if he were smashing china plates at a summer fair.

The other three released every animal they could find, "liberating" them to an uncertain fate. They were in and out in twenty-two minutes flat. Point made; job done. Headlines guaranteed.

Victoria Boosler even gave unsuspecting Reg 1 a wink on the way out. Thirteen minutes later she turned into an industrial estate and pulled up in the deserted car park where their actual vehicle, a small flat-back lorry, was parked. Vicky swiftly removed the blonde wig and stuffed it into a hold-all along with the darker one she'd used to hijack the van, the sky-blue contact lenses and her uniform which she replaced with a black Rancid t-shirt. Her own hair was short and brunette; and her eyes were hazel. She left the padded bra on for now.

Tim and Jake joined her upfront as Pete Harrison doused the stolen van in diesel and set it ablaze.

Pete was quite content to sit alone in the back. That had been close, he thought. A couple more slashes and the Doc would have been deader than a eunuch's groin.

This had been his first "mission" with SAC. He knew he was being tested and that it was a test he had to pass. He'd been hanging around the group's periphery for some time appearing at almost every demo, benefit gig and rabble-rousing meeting that they attended. It hadn't taken long to confirm that Tim Robb was a dangerous megalomaniac on a mission, with a strong streak of paranoia that wasn't helped by his copious drug consumption.

Robb was aligned to many causes, from the Greens to the Hunt Saboteurs, but word on the scene suggested that he was involved in a recent pipe bomb attack that had blinded a research scientist in Cambridge. Now SAC was his baby, and chaos was increasingly his business.

***

"So what did you make of our new recruit?"

"Very strapping, darling," Vicky said playfully.

"Handy with the bat as well," added Jake.

"He was right to stop you, Tim."

Robb nodded thoughtfully. "I thought he was bricking it, but he's actually quite bright... for an oik."

"How do we know him again?"

"Jake spotted him in action decking a couple of Hooray Henry fox-hunters and I quietly tapped him up."

"Terrific right hook," Jake added.

"And what do we know about him?"

"His real name's Pierre James Harrison. Working-class boy. From Eltham, some hole in south east London."

"Woh! A working-class boy called Pierre?" said Tim with a sneer.

"His mother's French-Canadian. He prefers Pete or PJ. He's had legit experience as a sab, with a criminal record to prove it, and his parents are life-long TUC and CND activists. Our man says it all checks out. It's all kosher. He's a vegan, moved down here for work, hates the Tories. A perfect soldier."

Victoria wanted to ask who had checked it out and how but thought better of it. "Good-looking too," she sighed.

"Careful Tim, you might lose her," laughed Jake. "Vee probably fancies a bit of rough."

"You know that's not true."

"Of course. But it wouldn't hurt if you got to know him a little better," said Robb. "Toy with him a bit. See if your Spidey senses pick up anything out of order."

"Oh, I do love a challenge."

***

Six Hours Later.

Pete Harrison had never seen anything like this. It was the biggest gathering of pond life this side of Lake Windermere. The old warehouse on the outskirts of Bristol was positively heaving with soap-dodgers, full-time spongers and the perpetually offended. There were student radicals, ageing punks, rent-a-mob protestors, dossing lecturers, well-spoken feminists, different shades of anarchists... He had already lost count of the number of white men with dreadlocks and clogs – *CLOGS!* – he had spotted.

What had Garry Johnson called them? *The sons and daughters of well-off bankers, Tom Robinson's army of trendy wankers.*

Suburban rebels playing at reds.

Pete sniffed. The smell of weed was so prevalent you could probably get high just by breathing in the air.

In the background an endless loop of the Ozric Tentacles' back catalogue slopped out of huge black speakers that had once belonged to a reggae sound system and still faintly bore the words 'Black Lion' in faded silver spray paint. Pete had forgotten which of the myriad of right-on radical groupings had organised this gathering. It didn't matter; they were all much of a muchness. He'd attended so many similar events recently that it was all just a succession of dirty streaks across his memory.

He sat back on an old, busted couch, nursing a can of Special Brew that he had liberated from a cool box, and accepted the dog-end of a joint which had just been passed to him by some patchouli-soaked crusty. He scanned the room casually. A handful of badly dressed punters were shuffling around close to the speakers in what passed for dancing, and there were a few like him just watching the world go by on other seats, some of which had clearly been rescued from nearby skips, along with battered beanie bags and upturned milk crates.

Most of the crowd were huddled around the room in conspiratorial groups passing doobies, swigging strong cider and talking shit. No doubt plotting new ways to bring the evil Establishment and its cronies to their knees, he thought.

Pete smirked and drew deeply on the final burning embers of the spliff. His stomach churned when he thought back to Tim Robb cutting that deep gash in the scientist's face. The crazy bastard would have finished him off without losing a minute's sleep. Every fibre in Pete's body had ached to beat

Robb to a pulp at that moment. But that would have blown everything.

He scanned the room and saw Tim laughing loudly with a group of his devotees and re-enacting today's action as he mimed vicious slashing motions with his hand.

Over to his left there were a handful of half-decent looking and relatively clean student women. Pete wondered how many pints it'd take before he made a move in their direction. Toffee-nosed totty wasn't his thing, but needs must when the devil drives and all that...

"You did well today, Harrison."

The voice, upper middle class to the core, belonged to Tim who beamed as he tapped his beer can against Pete's. "I thought you'd lost your bottle a bit but it all worked out in the end."

Pete looked at him evenly, noting his Eat The Rich t-shirt and tattered black Harrington jacket blemished with Crass badges.

"I'm Millwall, mate. It'd take more than a bit of claret to endanger my Aris. But in fairness, killing an unarmed old cunt is not considered good manners even down the Den."

Tim threw back his curly mane and laughed loudly.

"You were right; it would've been lousy propaganda, bad for the cause. But old, young, male, female...when the day comes it won't matter what they are if they're the enemy." He paused, searching for the right stolen quote, and found it. "You can't make an omelette without smashing a few eggs."

Or if you don't know your way around a hob, thought Pete. But he bit his tongue and nodded. "You're right there Tim." And yet you can barely utter a sentence without a cliché. What a fucking clown.

"Good man. You need any gear?"

Robb patted his pocket.

"I'm good with beer, thanks. When's the next outing?"

Tim laughed. "You are keen. We'll leave it a bit, long enough for security to get lax again and then" – he paused for dramatic effect and lowered his voice – "then we hit them with the biggest stunt to date, the one that'll make SAC front page news the whole world over."

He patted Pete's knee. "Now, where can I get a fuck in this place?"

"Prick," thought Pete as Robb staggered off in search of a class warrior with low standards, no bra, few discernible inhibitions and a high tolerance threshold for body odours. He was still simmering five minutes later when Victoria flopped down on the couch next to him. At least she smelt good.

Vicky's cheeks were flushed from dancing and judging by her pupils some recent class A stimulation. She was glowing and when her lower leg accidentally brushed against Pete's he felt a twinge of excitement.

"How are you, Mr Harrison? Enjoying the evening's festivities?" The music was so loud that she had leaned across the couch to make herself heard and Pete could feel her hot breath on his ear.

"Not really, Vicks."

He stared deeply into her eyes for the first time and realised he didn't want to look away. It was a lightning bolt moment. The attraction was instant. Primal. Mutual?

Pete glanced over to the dance floor where Tim was playing air guitar frantically along to a hard rock racket.

He leaned in to her. "I think I'd rather be somewhere more private...for a proper chat."

"God, I am so glad you said that." Victoria got to her feet in one fluid, feline motion. "I know just the place."

Boosler was a force to be reckoned with. Within five minutes she had commandeered a long-haired youth known as "Stone" to drive the pair of them to the nearest railway station in his rusty Citroen 2CV. There they bundled into the back seat of a taxi.

"College Fields, Clifton," Victoria barked imperiously at the driver. "Number fourteen."

The English upper class still know how to treat their inferiors, thought Pete.

As soon as the taxi was in motion, she patted Pete's knee and left her hand there.

"So, Stone?"

"Real name's Steve, but he was born at the Stonehenge Free Festival, eighteen or so years ago."

"He wasn't in charge of the disco, was he?"

"Ha. No idea. Not a fan of the Ozrics then?"

"Never even heard of 'em. Madness and Squeeze are more my cuppa tea."

"That figures. Not Iron Hammer then? They were playing just before we left, some frightful heavy metal shower. Tim's favourites."

"Not really. I'm more Grateful Dead than Motorhead when it comes to that kind of..."

The taxi driver swerved suddenly to avoid a cat and Victoria's hand slid along the inside of his right thigh, pausing just before the event horizon. She left it there for a beat too long. They kissed softly.

"Of thing," he added slowly. "Where are we going by the way?"

"My parents' house. Well, one of them. They're down at the Jersey pad this week. We've got the run of the place."

Her hand was back, above his knee. Pete patted it gently but nothing more. There was no rush.

"You seemed keen to get away."

"You haven't seen Timothy pissed yet, have you?"

Pete shook his head.

"He's a 'fun drunk' which essentially translates as he gets very loud, very annoying and acts extremely inappropriately. Air guitar was just the start."

"Remind me not to lace his herbal tea. Tell me about you."

"Open book, darling. Only child. Daddy's a trader, commodities not market stalls. Mother never needed to work. I boarded at Roedean, outside Brighton, and passed the entrance exam for Peterhouse...and..."

"You dropped out."

"Am I that readable? Yes, mummy and daddy were so very disappointed. I was supposed to land a rich Hooray Henry and fire out a few sprogs. Boring! So instead of studying bio-chemistry I started working in a research lab just outside of Reading...where my eyes were well and truly opened to the horrors within."

She leant over and kissed him on the cheek. "That was for helping out today."

He kissed her back, on the lips, meeting no resistance.

"You did pretty well yourself."

"Here we are, driver!"

The cabbie stopped abruptly and yanked heavily on his handbrake. Victoria leapt out leaving Pete to pay the £16 fare.

"And that," he told the driver as he flung him a £20 note. "Is how the rich stay rich."

Pete looked up at the towering, three-storey town house and felt like whistling. He had stayed in hotels smaller than this.

"Peter, come inside! You'll scare the neighbours. You look like a burglar casing the joint!"

The interior was as tasteful, immaculate and upper middle class as a show-home in Virginia Waters. Apart from a copy of yesterday's *Times* on the settee, not a thing was out of place.

Only one of the two of them knew that an Ultra Compact Pearlcorder L400 Micro would be recording every word that was spoken that evening.

Victoria steered him through to the open plan kitchen and poured them both a large brandy.

"Ta. I'll take a beer with mine, if you've got one."

She went to the massive fuck-off American fridge freezer and returned with a well-chilled Bud.

"So, Mr Harrison, it's your turn. Tell me about you."

"Open book, just like you. Only child, hard-working parents, academically challenged. I left Crown Woods in Eltham with no qualifications and ended up in the Royal Green Jackets."

"Which battalion?"

"3RGJ, over in Celle."

"Intriguing. So how did you get involved with politics?"

"Mum and dad were union people. Me old man used to flog the Morning Star in Eltham High Street sometimes. I wasn't interested. But some of the kids on our estate were in a band called Conflict, if you've heard of them" – she nodded – "They were anarchist punks. Crass school but much more down to earth. I knew Colin Jerwood well. They all liked a tear-up. Through them I got involved with the Hunt Sabs..."

"Admirable. How do you make a living?"

"Labouring mostly, and odd jobs for cash."

"Are you involved with any kindred organisations?"

"Are you a spy? No. Just you lot. I was floating about before I met Tim. He's quite a character. Does he often get schitzy?"

She lit a cigarette and took a drag that went on as long as her legs.

"Not with me," she said finally. "But the gozz is he slapped his last girlfriend around. And there was that scientist..."

A fruit machine jackpot lit up in Pete's head. This was exactly what he wanted to hear – and Victoria seemed more than willing to talk. But at the same time, he didn't want to seem over-eager. They had all night.

"You two loved up then?"

Victoria shrugged. "We're not exclusive."

She smiled and stepped towards him. Pete pulled her closer and they kissed each other hard. Her fingers immediately dropped to his cock, which she held, enjoying the rapid hardening.

Very forward these posh birds, he thought.

"I'm going upstairs to jump in the shower and change into something more comfortable. Can you open the bottle of Pouilly-Fuissé in the fridge please and make yourself at home?"

"Polly what?"

"The white wine."

Pete found the bottle – Fortnum & Mason – opened it after a struggle with the corkscrew and placed it in a silver ice bucket which he filled with ice. Then he poured the remainder of his Bud down the sink and went back to the front room to flick through the day-old copy of *The Times*.

When Victoria came down the stairs in a satin bathrobe fifteen minutes later, Pete Harrison was gone. The only sign that he'd even been there was an empty beer bottle, the open wine bottle, and yesterday's newspaper left open on the personal ads.

Victoria shrugged and turned off the Pearlcorder.

Chapter Four

It took ten minutes for Pete to become me, and another twenty for me to become someone else.

Pete wasn't really called Pete of course, let alone Pierre James Harrison, known as PJ to his non-existent family. The name was taken, as is usually the case, from the death certificate of a poor tot who had died aged just six weeks at the right time in the right place. Pete was just the latest "legend" I had adopted for my work.

I'm Harry Dean by the way, an undercover Metropolitan police detective. As I wasn't dealing with normal criminals on this job, I had put my preferred character – fast-talking Harry Tyler – on the back burner and opted for one more suited to the task in hand; although all the time I was Pete I was aware of how much my inner Tyler would love to drop Tim Robb with a well-aimed forearm smash to the jaw.

PJ was quieter and more sombre than wise-cracking Harry, and far less likely to rattle polite sensibilities. Every part of my new legend's back

44

story had been meticulously crafted. Pete Harrison had a passport, a birth certificate, a National Insurance number and legitimate-seeming bank accounts, not to mention the driving licence I had let Tim catch sight of. Peter Harrison's "fake" was more legit than a lot of the real people in the circle he was moving in. They were a strange breed and entitled to their opinions no matter how barmy they were, but there was good reason to suspect that some – or perhaps just one – of them were behind the unexplained disappearance of two local abattoir workers, as well as the pipe-bomb attack, and escalating animal rights violence in the area.

The smart money said it was Tim Robb.

Harry Tyler would have given Victoria Boosler what she clearly wanted right there on the back seat of the taxi. And then again on the kitchen floor. Pete played things differently. Victoria was Robb's confidante and his muse. She was the key to finding out what the next move was – so it could be stopped before it happened. My plan as Pete was to win her trust, but if her lust was part of the deal, so be it.

I had fully intended to let Pete pogger the granny out of the toffee-nosed bint that evening. Until I'd spotted the coded message in The Times – the only way my handler, DI Mark Nixson, can communicate with me. I called him from the first working phone box I found, and was picked up ten minutes later. By 3am I was in Didcot, in another woman's bed, and dreaming of what might have been.

The bed belonged to my great aunt Agatha who, unbeknown to her, stored several of my aliases in a concealed strongbox in the basement she never used. I arrived as Pete and left after four hours kip with Harry Tyler's passport, credit cards, mobile phone, driving licence and the £500 float. Aunt Agatha was none the wiser. She didn't even hear me open the garage that she never went in and drive out in a dark blue Ford Granada that she didn't know was parked there.

Harry Tyler was back.

***

May 19, 1990.

The Happy Eater Cafe could never be said to be Didcot's premier eating establishment, but thanks to its glamorous low-rent location on Station Road – jammed between the near derelict Labour Club and a crumbling factory unit – they could afford to serve generous platefuls of fried nosh at reasonable prices. Not for nothing was their Full English known locally as "The heart attack on a plate".

At 11am, it was too late for breakfast and too early for dinner – what the middle classes call lunch. But here that didn't matter. The menu was the same all day long, except for Christmas week when the seasonal special involving processed turkey, with or without a festive dollop of curry sauce, and over-boiled Brussels sprouts was available.

DCI Roy Pryor had made it his business to drive DI Shirley Kelly and DI Mark Nixson to the meeting. They were greeted by the sight of the Met's finest soldiering his way through the cafe's Super-Deluxe offer (£15 – or free if consumed in under twenty minutes…presuming your arteries didn't harden like cement in the process).

"Take it easy, Aitch, you're supposed to at least breathe in between mouthfuls,' said Nixson with a smirk.

"Sorry guv, I couldn't resist, I was Hank Marvin – I've been living on alfalfa and stinging nettles for weeks. I needed some proper nosebag."

I wiped a smear of Daddies Sauce from around my mouth, stood up and shook their hands. I knew my handler Mark Nixson pretty well. He was a working-class kid from Clitheroe in Lancashire with a rarely mentioned passion for Primal Scream. At first glance he looked like the sort of bloke who sells wills for a living, but he was quite tough and quietly ambitious.

Roy Pryor was old school, a proper copper, hard but avuncular. A detective out of time. Roy was apparently once the proud owner of the worst combover in the Met, but these days the few lonely wisps of hair he still possessed looked flimsier than a butterfly's nightie.

Shirley Kelly was new to me and instantly impressive, being a stunning and generously proportioned mixed-race woman. Shirley looked a bit like Pauline Black from The Selecter but sounded more like Pauline Quirke. Thirty-something would be my guess. 36C would be my next one. It took some effort to tear my blue eyes away from her green ones, but I managed it, looking over at Roy and rolling straight back into character.

"Every time I go to the khazi my arse is like the map on Bonanza. Still, who'd ever have thought eating a sausage would blow my cover?"

"Too much information," laughed Nixson.

"A deeply unpleasant image," said Shirley with a smile. "But if you're on the clock" – she nodded towards the poster advertising the Super-Deluxe challenge – "we can wait." ·

"A fiver says he'll do it," sniffed Pryor.

"A tenner says the cardiac arrest will kill him first. Any chest discomfort, dear?"

I clutched my chest and mimed life-threatening pain.

"Just a cockle, Shirl?" laughed Roy. "Many would pay a lot more to see our Harry peg it."

"What was it like being Pete Harrison rather than Harry Tyler?" Mark Nixson asked.

"If you think of it as method acting, Harry is always more fun. Between us, Peter is a bit of a dull cove."

"So Harry is your Hamlet?" said Shirley.

"I guess. But Hamlet without the bitterness and melancholy."

"More Macbeth?"

"More Falstaff... for the lechery."

She laughed.

"How are you getting on with that mob?" Nixson said quietly. "That business at the Benston Institute got a bit naughty, didn't it? A security guard beaten senseless, a scientist still in hospital...did it need to go that far?"

I swallowed a chunk of charred black pudding and sighed. "You know I'm still just the new boy, guv, I was lucky to even get in the room. But I stopped it going further. Believe me it could've been a whole lot worse. Comrade Tim is a fucking animal. But they trust me; I'm in with him and Victoria, the tight circle..."

Just how tight was her circle? I wondered. Odds on Pete Harrison would find out before the job was through.

"We've had a reliable tip that they are in the market for plastic explosives, some serious stuff. Do you know what that could be for?"

"Robb is definitely plotting something big. I'm not all the way into the loop yet but I'm getting there. They are suspicious bastards. If Pete had an old school tie, I could melt down the barriers quicker, but what can you do? I'm just their bit of muscle, a handy peasant to take care of all the shit jobs."

"Who are you closest to?"

"Boosler."

"So you'll be gently pumping her for information."

I suppressed a smile. "That's the plan, guv," I said straight-faced.

"Well, I'm sorry to pull you out early."

Was he doing this deliberately? Most unlike the DI. But there wasn't so much as a glimmer of a smile in those hard Lancashire features.

"Coppus Interruptus," said Shirley Kelly, who was obviously on top of the double meanings, making me like her even more.

"It's not a problem; they knew I was away this weekend for a visit home. It's no big deal to throw in a family tragedy to explain the fact that I have to hang around a bit longer and sort out the repercussions. They'll buy it."

I paused and tapped the table. "This must be big then."

"Big yes," said Roy Pryor. "And personal to a degree. Shirley here will fill you in."

I nodded and triumphantly scooped the remains of the fried eggs up with the last piece of toast with one minute and fifty-seven seconds on the clock.

"One cardiac su un piatto… finito," I said in cod Italian.

Shirley Kelly reluctantly handed Roy Pryor a cockle.

"You treat your body like West Ham treated Wolves," she said disapprovingly.

"That's as may be," I said with a smile. "But I'm still a long way from injury time."

***

I have to admit I felt sick. I had seen a lot of dead men, but the sight of Mark Brennan's mutilated corpse was something else. The bastards hadn't just killed a police officer, they had autographed the crime and then underlined it by raping a woman they thought was his widow and, in the process, effectively murdered what they thought was his unborn child.

The only positive was it betrayed an arrogance that, unchecked, would become a weakness.

I was sitting in the back of Roy Pryor's Daimler Sovereign with Shirley Kelly. Pryor and Mark Nixson were in the front seats.

"Highly irregular, but…" Roy had said.

"But local plod are that bent?"

"Riddled," said Shirley.

"Shot through with dry rot," added Pryor. "We can't trust any of them. If they get a sniff of you, you're as good as dead."

"The one factor in my favour being the Bishops wouldn't think we'd have the brass balls to try again this quickly."

"That's exactly our thinking, Harry."

49

Shirley showed me a collection of pictures of the band and the Iron Hammer "crew".

"This one is Mungo, he's pure evil, even uglier inside than out," she said, holding up a close-up of Don Warwick.

"A Nightmare On Elm Street," said Pryor.

"A nightmare on any street," replied Shirley.

"I know him," I said.

"How?"

How? I'll never forget that nasty bastard. I was in a West Ham pub in Plaistow, High Street early one Monday. I think the Victoria Tavern. It was about five-ish so it wasn't busy. I was up at the bar, sipping a lager and reading the sports page, and I was aware of Warwick making a nuisance of himself. He was a big lump but as pissed as a pallet of puddings. He could barely talk. A young girl came in with a mate. Pretty young thing, looked a bit like Dannii Minogue, but sounded more Bow Bells. She was celebrating her 18th, she said, although I suspected it was more likely to have been her 17th. Maybe even 16th. Warwick made a wobbly beeline for the two of them and offered to buy them a drink. The birthday girl politely turned him down. Clearly disgruntled, Warwick stumbled over to the jukebox, fumbled for a pound coin and made his selections. 'Peaches' by the Stranglers started to sleaze from the speakers.

"Stand on the table," he told her. She refused. "Come on, dance for me." It was an order, not a request.

That was when I had a really good look at him. His eyes were small, piggy even, and dull, but he was built like a prize fighter, broad and strong. Even three parts plastered I knew he would be a proper handful.

The girl's boyfriend arrived and asked Warwick to leave them alone. Mungo put the smaller, younger man in a fierce headlock. I remember he had a beer bottle in his hand, light ale I think, and he didn't spill a drop. The barmaid said "Oi!" and another young kid started to move towards him. Warwick growled at them and they both backed off.

"Stand up!" he snapped at the tearful teenager. She did as she was told because she could see her boyfriend was in pain. "Take your clothes off and dance for me or we'll see how long it takes for me to snap lover boy's neck."

She started dancing. "Clothes off, on the table!" he snapped. "Then you can do some tricks for me with this." He drained the bottle and put it on the table. "Better to lose yer cherry to a light ale than this fucking milkshake."

The poor girl was in tears.

"He was causing a nuisance in a pub," I replied finally.

"Would he recognise you?"

"No, I don't think so."

Not unless he had eyes in the back of his head. I don't think he even saw the pool cue coming at him. One good wide swing from the right side. Knocked him sparko. The girl was on the table by then, dancing in tears. I helped her down, helped her boyfriend up, and escorted them to the door. "You'll have a better time in the Black Lion," I said quietly. "This place ain't fit for human beings. Too many unpleasant smells."

The few scattered punters and the barmaid gave me a round of applause. I didn't deserve it. I wasn't proud of knocking out a man from behind, but sometimes the easy way is the better way,

I told the barmaid to direct any teenagers to the other pub. She wanted to buy me a drink, but I had things to do.

"Are you positive?"

"There's no way he'd remember me."

"That's a relief. That would have jeopardised the job before we had even started."

Shirley went back to her pictures. "This is one is known as One-Gin, shortened to 'Wungy', who is basically the brothers' go-fer."

More hard cases and ugly bugs followed in quick succession: Spider, black Chad Matthews, Jimmy "The Crank" Kossler, the angry looking Psycho Manny… all tough enough to cause problems. Except for one, a tubby, soft-faced man who looked like Penfold from the kids TV cartoon series Danger Mouse.

"Who's that?"

"Henry Gibson, on paper he's their manager although Terry makes all the musical decisions. Gibson was a contract lawyer. He handles the fine print with record labels and publishers, advises on investments and keeps the businesses they own looking legit."

I nodded. "And this older guy, who's he?"

"Victor Galanis, their road manager, but also a mentor from day one. He's not about so much now. He had pleurisy back in February and is likely to retire soon, we think. Vic had connections to older East End crime families like the Dixons and the Lambrianous."

"Georgie Dixon was the one. Do they have other organised crime links?"

"Yes. The Knights are family. They go back a long way."

"Big players. And Custom House?"

"A good working relationship. They don't tread on each other's toes. They're well thought of in Islington and by the Rainham old firm too."

I looked at the pictures of the brothers.

"Are there only two of them?"

"They had a sister," said Shirley. "Rosie. She was younger."

"Was?"

"Teenage suicide. She was sixteen. The gossip around it, very whispered gossip, was that the poor girl was being repeatedly abused, either by Wolf or by both of them. She never came to us of course, and her close friends at school would never talk to anyone about it. You know how it is. Now this could all just be malicious gossip, but it tells you something about these men that people around them believe them capable of something so evil."

"Parents alive?"

"The mother is," said Nixson. "Horrible woman. She looks like Medusa having a bad hair day. She's fairground stock. Claims to be Romany."

"The father, Big Terry, worked for Bernie Silver," added Shirley. "The bad genes go back generations."

"They are nasty bastards, Harry," cautioned Roy Pryor. "And they will be hard to get close to. They're a very tight-knit gang."

"How did Mark get in?"

"He went the football route."

"ICF?"

"The Mile End Mob."

"Do we know why they moved away from the Tom, from the jewellery heists?"

"They're making so much from record sales, live concerts and merchandise that they don't need to take the risk," explained Shirley. "They're booked for a massive US tour this Autumn opening for Metallica. Ever since MTV put 'Love Bumps' on heavy rotation last year, they've been played to death on college radio."

I snorted. 'Love Bumps'. As subtle as a jackhammer. But shit sells, I guess. "They still run drugs?"

"Yes, according to our sources. It involves less jeopardy but it's still lucrative; handy cash – it pays for the entourage and gets washed easily in the businesses they own. We could bust the pubs and clubs for MDMA and cocaine, but that wouldn't close down the Bishops. We wouldn't catch the brothers hands on."

"And even if we did, it's not what we want to prosecute them for," said Roy. "They're murderers, people smugglers, rapists..." He paused, and bit his lower lip softly before adding the single word "Scum."

"They're a tumour," said Mark Nixson. "And you don't treat a tumour with sticking plasters."

"Any known weaknesses?"

"Apart from the class As? The usual. Vanity, women. Terry is married – to his second wife, Sylvia – but it doesn't stop him tomcatting around. Wolf is rumoured to swing both ways..."

"There was a teenage fling with a local boy whose parents were bought off," said Roy. "Old enough to be legal, young enough to be creepy. Those rumours of bi-sexuality linger on and most of the firm aren't keen on that or on him."

"And if we're trading in gossip, the word is Mungo gets off on cross dressing," added Shirley.

"There's an image to keep kids away from the fireplace," chortled Mark Nixson.

"We have heard that the brothers fall out occasionally. There's talk of full-on fights backstage. The usual sibling rivalries, amplified by ego and wealth. Their tempers are notorious."

"And what are you doing about the bent cop connections?"

"We're getting phone taps into all of the Bishops' main businesses," said Roy. "We haven't got the manpower for covert surveillance at this stage."

I wasn't impressed. These were clever, cunning criminals; in all probability any incriminating exchanges would be done face to face rather than over the phone.

"Get anything?" I asked hopefully.

"Only Mungo on a sex line."

I suppressed a laugh. "Did he call them or has he set up one of his own?"

Shirley smiled. "Talk ugly to me," she suggested.

"Really, guv, we need someone to infiltrate Stratford nick," I mused.

"That needs authorisation from someone higher up the payroll, but that's a future option," said Roy, adding hesitantly "If need be."

If need be? He means, if I fuck up. Or worse, luck out. I must have looked unsure because Nixson asked "Are you worried about the job, Harry?"

"Only that Iron Hammer's massed ranks of stage lights might trigger epilepsy," I said, faking total confidence.

I thought for a moment. "Do we know what the band have got lined up?"

Shirley handed me their tour schedule.

"They're billing these gigs as the second half of their summer 'Cut The Grass' tour but there are only four dates left now.

Swindon, Coventry, Ipswich and then back to Stratford Town Hall for the grand finale."

I grunted.

"But tonight, they are here."

She produced a badly printed flyer. "It's a bikers' benefit gig in east Middlesex."

"Near Southall?"

"Four or five miles out."

I studied the flyer and smiled. I'd had worse plans.

Chapter Five

Middlesex

Four hours later, I left the Old Oak Tree Inn in Southall. My head was shaved, my clothes were football casual – Lacoste top and trainers, navy cargo strides – and the grin on my lips was as empty as the suitcase in my hand. This was a long shot but right now it was all I had.

The scrap yard was a short bus ride away. It had been nearly four years since I'd worked there with the notorious Potman and Noodles; or rather since I had finished my undercover initiation period there. The two rogues had never seen through me and we'd parted company on good terms, which meant I was able to use their names as a handy reference with impunity.

If anyone would have an in to a local bikers' gig, it would be the man mountain Hells Angel known as Potman.

***

The massive scrap yard looked almost exactly the same as when I'd first seen it in August 1986, with ugly mounds of clapped-out fridges and redundant washing machines vying for the eye with rows of useless cars; all waiting to be crushed or cut – more accurately burnt with blow torches – to furnace size.

There was only one problem. The gates were firmly chained shut. Where the fuck had Little and Large got to? Panicking slightly, I strolled round to their grotty local, The Red House. They were probably in there, or if not, someone there would know.

Guns N' Roses' 'Paradise City' was playing incongruously as I waited for the barmaid to pull my pint; the rock-packed Seeburg jukebox was still the best thing about the place. I was admiring her cleavage when a hand playfully grabbed my crotch from behind.

"If you're searching for drugs they're in me right-hand pocket," I said.

"Harry!" a young woman squealed with delight. "It's been years."

I turned and looked her over. My assailant was fit, curvy, and dressed head to toe in black leather.

"Eggy? Is that you?"

She beamed.

"But look at ya. You used to look like a dippy hippy, now you're more like Joan Jett."

"I'm Janine again now and I'm all grown up, Harry." She pulled me closer and whispered, "Now, I'm legal."

I groaned inwardly as I thought back to the late-night blow job Noodles's daughter had given me years before in the backseat of a doomed Cortina. She had been fifteen years and ten months old at the time, but I knew the "she looked older" defence wouldn't have held much water then... or now.

Right on cue Aerosmith's 'Jailbait' started up on the jukebox, as if the universe itself was taking the piss.

"You're even more gorgeous," I smiled, and I actually meant it too.

"Why thank you, kind sir."

"Is yer dad about?"

"No, the Chuckle Brothers are in Minorca buying a lovely fuck-off villa just down the road from Jimmy Jones's place."

"Kinnell. Well, that's a bugger. I thought they might know about this Iron Hammer gig tonight."

"That's where we're going," – she indicated two more hot, leather-clad young women on a table by the window. "That's why we're all dolled up. Hey, you could come with. You can be my plus one."

"There's a guest list for a charity show?"

"Dad helped organise it. It's for their new clubhouse. It's right next to their old one, and as soon as you see it you'll know why they need a new one. Think of it as a favour. You can do me one later...if you're good."

I smiled broadly and kissed her on the lips. "Love ya, Eggs. Sorry, love ya, Janine. Of course I'll come with ya, but I'll sling a score in the collecting bucket anyway. And I'll pick you girls up and drive us there, if you like."

She cuddled me again. "I'd like that...and later, a ride for a ride."

"In your Magic Bus?"

"Yeah. I'll punch your ticket," she giggled. "Standing room only."

***

The gig was taking place on an actual working farm, although the small cattle herd had been moved to a neighbouring farmstead three quarters of a mile away to escape the ear-bleeding noise, leaving only the poor cow behind the bar.

A sturdy but compact stage had been constructed in one of the cow sheds. I reckoned it would comfortably hold 200 people; but the stage was also visible from the rear of the shed and from stage left. The mixing desk was at the very back, behind where the audience would be.

The crew's work rate would certainly put any of the old London dockers to shame. I was impressed. The rows of impeccably maintained motorcycles – Harleys of course, alongside Honda RC30s, Norton Commandos and a pristine Ninja 900 – looked the business too.

Across the field I clocked a small sea of tents and to the left of the clubhouse there was a chow wagon and a decent-sized beer tent.

"Come on," said Janine. "The clubhouse is the 'backstage' area; it's where the after party will be. Come and meet Mungo."

Him, already!

From twenty feet away, Don Warwick looked like a big man; up close, he was stockier and uglier than I'd remembered. He looked like a horror film had lost its monster. Mungo had oily black hair, weasel eyes and a hooter that had been squashed and bent like plasticine. His teeth were yellow stumps. His wide face was scarred and battered from countless battles, some in the ring, most out of them. His left cheek bore the permanent pattern of a jagged pint glass and he had a raised vein on the side of his head that seemed to throb.

There didn't appear to be any visible snooker cue scars.

Mungo had a face that would give Luca Brasi nightmares. Yet Janine jumped into his arms and planted a kiss right on it.

"Mungo!" she squealed.

"Eggy darlin'! How's yer old man?"

"He's fucked off to El Castell with Noodles. But I've got a new daddy to mind me."

Mungo gave me a hard stare.

"It's all right, he's one of yours."

"How's that?"

"He's West Ham."

Eggy walked into the club house. I held out a hand; Mungo left it hanging.

"South London West Ham," I said pleasantly.

"I thought I could smell something."

A bit rich, I thought, considering Mungo's breath possessed the kind of odour you might reasonably associate with Dennis Nielsen's cellar. I had been around enough headcases to know instinctively that Warwick was pure evil.

"Oi Plumstead, d'you know this ice cream?"

Mark Corrigan of the ICF walked over.

"He says he's a South London Hammer."

Corrigan gave me the once-over. "Yeah? Who d'you know?"

"Fatty Lol, Fitzy, Lewisham..."

"Proper people." Even a chump like Mungo couldn't miss the respect in his voice.

"I'm from Essex originally but I was grafting around Lee Green for years. I've seen you in the Northy, ain't I?" I said, referencing the Lord Northbrook pub.

"You would have done, mate."

"So you must know Whaley? And Steve Cooper?"

"'Course." The man known as Plumstead beamed. I carried on, "What about that time Steve Cooper had his own night bus service?"

Now Plumstead started laughing; Mungo looked blank. I ran with it.

"Steve came out of Lewisham station, as pissed as a thousand sailors on shore leave, saw a 261 bus standing empty with its engine running, climbed into the driver's cab..."

"And drove it home to Horn Park Lane," Plumstead finished my sentence gleefully. "Fucking legend! All these poor bastards with their arms out trying to flag it down and Stevie's driven straight past 'em..."

"Only occasionally veering up onto the pavement..."

"In fairness it was the only time the fuckin' bus ran on time."

Plumstead gave me an impromptu cuddle. Inwardly I breathed a sigh of relief. I'd passed the first test.

"I'll leave you girls to reminisce," shrugged Mungo. He walked off to the clubhouse.

"Thank you Mr Joie de fucking Vivre," muttered Plumstead.

"He's probably got stuff on his mind," I said affably.

"Oi Harry, let's get a pint," said Janine, emerging with some tell-tale white powder around her right nostril. "Over at the beer tent for now cos the boys are having a band meet. We'll catch up with them after the show."

I shook Plumstead's hand. "Laters, mate."

"Yeah, pleasure to meet ya, Aitch."

***

The gig was good, at least as much as it as I saw. After the first four numbers of raucous, bone-crushing heavy rock, Janine was tugging at my arm.

"I've got something you need to see," she hollered in my right ear. I thought about saying no, but Eggy was clearly my way in so I nodded and followed her reluctantly over to an old stone out-building.

"It's the milking parlour," she said solemnly.

"Great. But why are we here?"

"Because," she said, slowly unzipping my flies, "I need to demonstrate my milking techniques..."

Here we go! She 'milked' me twice; first orally, and then by riding me long and hard on the wooden floor. By then the music had stopped.

"Enough?" I asked.

"For now..." she said with a smile. "Now come on, we're missing a party, and I need to see my sweet old Uncle Charlie."

"You're gonna ruin that pretty schnozz of yours. Carry on snorting and it will melt away like a snowman in the Sahara."

"I don't care darling, daddy can afford a bit of cosmetic repair work for his only daughter. Besides, I'm here for a good time, not a long time."

The old "hope I die before I get old" bollocks. The Who had a lot to answer for. Not me, I want to die so old Methuselah would be green with envy.

We were the last ones to arrive at the after-show bash in the bikers' bar. The place was, of course, an unglorified shit-hole; the ceiling was stained yellow from years of cigarette smoke and joints, the walls were blitzed with tatty tour posters, motorbike spreads and soft porn pictures torn from Penthouse and Razzle, and what bare plaster you could see was covered in grime or large dents. At least the fridges were well-stocked.

Aerosmith's 'Love In An Elevator' blasted out of the Pioneer speakers, inspiring a couple of leather-clad lovelies to act out the "going down" line on their men-folk with an enthusiasm only half a bottle of vodka could generate. I gratefully grabbed a can of cold Stella while Janine waltzed off to socialise.

It was easy for me to separate the Iron Army from the bikers – length of hair, dress sense, aftershave. The East London firm combined nonchalant aggression with beery bonhomie, but the underlying threat of extreme violence was constant. These were hard men, proper monkey bastards. Men whose smiles would morph into masks of hate at the drop of a hat. Jack or otherwise.

I recognised two of them from the photos that Shirley Kelly had shown me: Jimmy "The Crank" Kossler and the ever-furious Psycho Manny with his face like a clenched fist. I could see Terry Bishop holding court on the other side of the clubhouse, Mungo was drinking whisky at the far end of the bar glaring at everybody – a psychopath wrapped in an idiot swathed in a moron – and I located Plumstead in a corner snogging Eggy's friend Shona in her tight Twisted Sister top. 'We're not gonna take it', read the slogan, but odds on she would.

Then I spotted someone else. A few feet from the edge of Terry's audience, a lone biker with unkempt brown hair and wild eyes was staring intently at Wolfy. His hand was inside the pocket of his army surplus camouflage jacket. He was gripping something.

This wasn't good.

John Mummery moved purposefully towards his target. The something in his jacket was a .38 Special. He knew he could get Wolfy, maybe Terry too. They weren't far apart. It would depend on how the crowd reacted to the first shot. He gripped the pistol tighter. He could do this. His heart was beating faster. Fear bubbled up inside his guts. But he had worked out his exit route and the ten grand prize was right there in front of him. He needed it. He would do it. He would do it now...do it! Do it!

The pistol was barely out of his pocket when a fist smashed into the left side of his jaw, knocking him off course. The gun was in his hand but before he could focus it on his attacker, the crop-haired twat hit him with another hard right that knocked Mummery clean off his feet. Then the man was on him, his knees pinning his arms down as his fists rained blows into his face. The music was cut, women were screaming. John Mummery was aware of the taste of his own blood before he passed out.

Terry Bishop, who had seen the whole scene unfold, reached us before Mungo could and eased me off the unconscious intruder.

"Easy, guy, easy. That cunt is out for the count." He looked me up and down and griped the bicep of my left arm. "I don't know you, but thank you."

His accent was so East London it could have been scraped off a wharf at St Katharine Docks.

"This is Harry," said Janine proudly.

"He's South London West Ham..." Mungo chimed in.

Bishop nodded, let go of my arm and offered me his hand to shake. "You know Fatty Lol, then?"

"He's Northbrook, he knows them all," said Plumstead, who was keen to be associated with the evening's hero. "This man is different gravy, Tel. He's as sound as a pound."

"I thought you were gunna fuckin' kill the dirty cunt," laughed Terry, patting my back.

Well, I might have done. I was trained to think fast and act faster.

"Lovely right hook, son," he added.

Up close, Terry Bishop didn't look much. He was an inch or two shorter than I was, but wider and wirier. I'd put him at thirteen stone, maybe thirteen and a half; and five will get you ten that a lot of that weight was muscle. His eyes were hard and intense, and right now they were darting about, looking for someone.

"Give us a minute."

Bishop pulled Mungo to one side and summoned One-Gin. The three men spoke quietly but intently for no more than a minute. Then Terry raised his voice and addressed the entire room. "Right," he said. "Change of plans gentlemen, we are driving on to Swindon tonight. Mungo, scrape this shit off the floor, drag him out and find out what that was about. Then give him a petrol shower and park him by a fire."

I shuddered inside but didn't let it show. He wasn't joking. They would slaughter the rogue biker as casually as you or I might brush a fly off of a sleeve.

If I could get to a phone box... but no, there were none for miles and my absence would be noticed. Maybe I could say something... but what? I couldn't do anything to arouse suspicion. Fate had dealt me a winning hand. I was in. I couldn't risk blowing it.

Terry Bishop slung a strong arm around me. His eyes had relaxed. "Come over and have a real drink with the chaps. Beer or whisky?"

"Stella's good, ta."

Terry handed me an ice cold can. "Charlie's on the Betty", he said casually as he waved his hand towards a fold-up table topped with king-size lines of cocaine.

"Ta, maybe in a bit. The old jam tart is still going nineteen to the dozen."

Terry grinned. "And understandably so; so, what brings you to this bucolic shit-hole?"

I shrugged. "I was in the area for a trade, bumped into Janine and here we are."

"Eggy? Worth bumping into. You know her old man then?"

"I did some work for them a few years back."

"Proper people. I like you even more. Did you, ah, ever get dippy with Eggy?"

I looked at him hard. "She told me she was older. I'm not proud of it."

Bishop laughed. "Now in normal circumstances after a confession like that you would be known as 'Bacon Bonce' or Harry the Child Catcher forever and a day, but I can't do that to a geezer who just saved me brother's life, can I?"

I grinned and then got serious. "What was that about? Did you know him?"

"No, but I don't think he was a spurned boyfriend." He laughed and spoke more softly. "Five will get you ten he was working for a little mob of unwashed wannabe Hells Angels out of Camberley who call themselves the Gypsy Rebels and foolishly see us as rivals... and if I'm right, and I usually am, they are about to find out that they are comprehensively out of their league."

I correctly took that to mean retaliation would be swift, public and brutal.

"An iron fist with the Iron Hammer."

He grinned. "It's the only way to be. He who has the hardest fist is remembered longest."

"Mohammad Ali?"

"Benito Mussolini. If someone threatens us, they get ripped apart. It's how we have to be in our game. Nobody gets to take the piss... except us."

I nodded in silent agreement. What else could I do? His face lightened up.

"Listen Aitch, we're going to fuck off now. We've got the Brunel Rooms in Swindon tomorrow night and I'd rather kip there tonight than face the M4 tomorrow. You're welcome to come along as our guest though. Jump on the tour bus now if you fancy it. We'll comp you a room."

"Cheers, I appreciate that. I've got a bit of graft to finish off around here, but how about I drive down to the show tomorrow night?"

"No problem, you're on the guest list, and the offer of a room still stands. We'll have a proper drink tomorrow."

"Shall I bring Janine?"

"Mate, you will not need to..."

Bishop looked around the club-house and lowered his voice. "We normally attract a better class of Richards than this. Look at that thing" – he nodded towards a sixteen stone biker woman with make-up worthy of a Halloween fright mask. "I'd sooner dry hump a sand dune... No, come on your Tod, bruv. You'll be fucking the brains out of a Page 3 bird tomorrow."

I smiled. "Or maybe into her..."

Bishop laughed, proving that there's nothing wrong with pressing an old joke into service every now and then.

***

Half an hour later I watched Iron Hammer's luxury single-decker sleeper bus reverse to a shuddering halt outside the club house. The band clambered on board, vanishing out of sight, along with both of Janine's hot, skinny friends. All of the bus's windows were blacked out. I went back into the club house, retrieved Janine from a biker's lap and walked her to the Granada. As I poured her onto the backseat, I clocked Mungo and a couple of other lumps setting off in a transit van with a biker escort. They looked like men on a mission and, as it happened, they were.

***

The next morning, I drove many miles out of my way to Bishops Green making sure I didn't have a tail. Once I was there, I rang Mark Nixson from a pay phone.

"Boss, I'm in."

"Already?"

"Fortune favours the brave."

"Need anything?"

"Not yet."

"Listen, there's some bad news. Catherine O'Mara died last night."

"From her injuries?"

"From a morphine overdose."

"Fuck."

"Only she wasn't on morphine. She only came round two days ago. She was hazy to start with but yesterday she told a WPC we sent in that she remembered what one of her attackers had looked like – the one who had come to the door initially. The others wore balaclavas. We were due to send a sketch artist down today."

"Don't tell me, the word must have leaked out of Stratford nick?"

"No. We don't think so. In fact, I'm almost certain this wasn't a police leak. The WPC is a good'un and she was reporting directly to Roy."

"It's quite a coincidence, though. But..." I thought for a moment. "It didn't need to be bent Old Bill," I said finally. "They could have bunged someone at the hospital. A nurse, a porter, another patient even...anyone. Offered 'em a monkey to ring when she comes round. That's what I'd have done."

"You think like they do, Harry."

"I have to."

***

I spent the afternoon reading the notes Shirley Kelly had given me. Some of the band's escapades were so outrageous you wouldn't believe them if they weren't in police reports. A gig on the outskirts of Manchester in 1986 turned into a pitched battle when Iron Hammer and their entourage of headcases, thugs and thieves saw off a much larger contingent of rockers, skinheads and hard punks. Unusually the locals were comprised of Man United and Man City supporters. In the papers and on TV and radio, the conflict was reported as being a football-related clash. In reality it was the brutal climax of a drug turf war.

Other small affrays had been sparked by the band's presence alone. Iron Hammer's reputation went before them like a battering ram, and every small-town hard man was keen to test out the Iron Army when the opportunity arose... Back in the early days, when they were playing pubs and clubs, it arose often.

According to a sycophantic write-up in *Kerrang!* – under the headline *Harder Than The Rest* – the Iron Army firm had gone toe to toe with headcases from Plymouth to Perth and had barely lost a drum stick in the process. But it was easy to talk up violence on a typewriter and dress it up as some grand cultural expression of working-class bravado, and quite another thing to be on the receiving end of it.

Perhaps more disturbing was a report about a hooker from Birmingham called Margaret Miller who had been hospitalised after a night with Terry Bishop. He had beaten her unconscious in a Sparkbrook guest house with his stage bullet belt. When she arrived at casualty, her body was found to be covered in small knife cuts and cigarette burns – Bishop is alleged to have told her "I don't like you, you're a bleeder". Miller later withdrew all charges saying that the sex had been consensual and that she had triggered his sadism by picking up his bullet belt after sex and saying, "Do you know how to use this? Do you know how to use it on me?"

Chapter Six

Iron Hammer's crowd warm-up music was instructive, I thought – 'Iron Maiden' by Iron Maiden, 'Radar Love' by Golden Earring, 'We Are The Firm' by the Cockney Rejects, Rose Tattoo's 'Scarred For Life' and finally Charlie Drake's 'My Boomerang Won't Come Back'. You could feel the excitement building through the sold-out audience, many of whom were beaming with expectation. As the final notes faded, the pitch-black stage was flooded with lights revealing the band in all their peacock glory as they slammed straight into the opening roar of 'Biffo' – their fast-paced tribute to John Bindon, which was as close to Motorhead as they ever sounded.

There were fifteen numbers in their set, that ranged in feel from the aggressive AC/DC style stomp of 'Bitch Trouble' to the puffed-up progressive rock of 'Profession Of Violence' via the playful 'Dalston Devil'. The latter featured the band's trademark demon, a masked figure known as BeelzeBob, normally acted out by One-Gin Denny. (It was why he needed that one large gin, he told me later. He couldn't go on stage without a shot of Dutch courage.)

The best numbers, to my mind, were 'Fort Vallance' – drivelling Kray Twins worship, yes, but with intricate twin guitar play so dazzling that it brought Thin Lizzy to mind – and the inevitable encore of 'Iron Hammer' itself, a raw, punk-metal all-guns-blazing romp with a chorus that was catchier than razor wire.

It was the quality of the songs and the standard of musicianship that surprised me most. Okay, they weren't The Jam but they weren't Emerson, Lake and Palmer either. They hit hard, their songs had proper hooks and they could really play. Terry's leads were exceptional, occasionally even skirting around the edges of sublime.

The show itself was pure spectacle. Electric theatrics. They had an impressive light show, operated by a guy from Dalston nicknamed Denny Lights, coupled with fireworks, smoke and stage craft. The most striking prop was a six-foot replica of a tormented human face which gushed out copious amounts of blood from the throat during the ominous 'Cut The Grass'.

It was a long way from the blues to be sure, but it obviously worked. The place was packed to the rafters.

One-Gin sent my new mate Mark 'Plumstead' Corrigan to meet me by the busy merch stand after the show and escort me to a near-by upmarket nightclub owned by "a business associate". Clearly a loaded one. The after-show do took up the entire upstairs bar, with a free bar and tables of high-end buffet nosh that stretched the entire length of the room. There was lobster, caviar, lasagne-stuffed peppers... not a vol-au-vent or sausage roll in sight.

The first thing I clapped eyes on was a naked fat bloke on all fours being led around on a diamanté-studded lead by a very tall and very stunning black woman. She was naked except for a black corset, black thigh-high boots and a thick, black nine-inch dildo poking out from her groin.

Dildo aside, she looked magnificent.

Dildo inside would hurt. Like buggery, I'd imagine.

"No prizes for guessing where that's gonna end up," laughed Plumstead. "That geezer's the chairman of the local council," he added. "Very useful when it comes to the old planning permission..."

"Bummer," I said.

"No, she'll bum him... And if the fat sap likes it up the jacksie from a high-class whore, then who are we mere mortals to judge? Especially when there is an actual judge over there on the top table..."

Plumstead nodded to an enclave sealed off by a rope. I glanced in his honour's direction and tried to keep the disgust off my face. Another flabby hypocrite.

"She's Tasmin, by the way," he added.

"Who are these Richards?" I asked, nodding at a group of glamorous women at the bar. A casual glance was enough to tell me that the clobber that they were half-wearing had cost each of them more than my old man used to earn in a month. One was sporting a silk-satin kaftan that looked like an Emilio Pucci.

"Models," said Plumstead. "That one on the far left was on Page 3 of *The Sun* today, but the way I hear it you'll need a bag of sand to rump it."

"If her nipples were any harder you could use them as an Etch-a-Sketch."

Plumstead laughed. "They're harder than fuckin' Rambo."

"They all on the game then?"

"No, some just like cock. So they help 'em out when they get busy. But see the bird with her feet at ten to two?" – he nodded towards a Rubenesque brunette. "She's got a fanny like an empty headlock, so best swerve her mate unless you're built like Buck Adams. Like rattling a stick around a bucket."

I laughed.

"And see that one there" – he indicated a heavy-breasted bottle blonde by the bar. "Her muscle control is out of this world. She can spray a geezer's cum across the room like a lawn sprinkler."

"And they said party tricks were dead."

"Well, it beats pebble-dashing."

"I know a bird who wipes her fanny with bleach," I said straight-faced.

"Yeah?"

"Flash cunt."

That made him roar. You have to know your audience. With Plumstead no joke was too low. In another life he might even have been good company.

"Hey look, Aitch," he said finally. "One-Gin told me to take you back-stage."

"There's another room?"

"Yeah. The big boys' room. It's supposed to be just for the band to chill a bit after the gig before the party starts, but Terry said to let you know that you can join them. I think he wants to chat."

I didn't react but inside I was glowing. Trust and inclusion. That's what this job is all about. Getting in and keeping in.

***

Moments later I pushed open the door to the private room and grinned. The "chill-room" looked more like a Ken Russell take on a Roman orgy. Talk about depravity. There was no mother-humping or granny-schtupping as far as I could tell, but pretty much every other vice was being indulged in, including fat white lines of Colombia's most lucrative export. Killers and thieves living like kings. There was enough unrestrained testosterone in the room to launch a small war. But the big positive was I was here, in the inner circle as an invited guest. Not an outsider.

'Bad Company' by Bad Company was playing over some hastily erected speakers – *'I was born a six-gun in my hand, behind the gun, I'll make my final stand'*.

Good lyrics. Maybe even prophetic.

Terry Bishop had his broad back to me, sampling the blow. To his right, Halfwit the drummer was hammering a pinball machine. I poured myself a JD and coke and looked around in time to see Wolf wince slightly as a voluptuous red-head took almost all of his cock deep into her mouth before locking into a rhythmic, slurping motion. He gave a low moan of heart-felt pleasure.

"Look at her go," said Terry who had materialised by my side, wiping his nose. "She could French kiss a moose with them lips. She's Welsh, or at least she sounded Welsh. It's hard to tell what with Bristol being such a rich stew of alien cultures."

I grinned.

"Here, fancy popping out to the tour bus for a bit, until the party warms up?"

I nodded. At that moment Wolf came with a grunt in the Welsh woman's mouth. She swallowed it theatrically, swishing it around her mouth first.

"You mean it gets hotter than this?"

"Fuck yeah. Wait till we're back the hotel. We make Led Zeppelin look like fuckin' choir boys."

Yeah, I thought, and Peter Grant look like Frank Spencer.

The Welsh bird headed towards us aiming for the shots.

"What's your name, love?" asked Terry.

"Myfanwy," she said reluctantly after a slight pause.

Terry smirked a little and then stroked the girl's hair gently, as if he actually gave a fuck. "Is that all I get, what about your surname?"

Myfanwy looked at him suspiciously.

"He's got to ask, love," I said with a smile. "Just in case you're a long-lost Bishop."

"Yeah, there are enough fucking inbred hillbillies in his clan already," laughed Terry.

"Hitchin. My second name is Hitchin," sighed the girl with a sense of defeat.

"Myfanwy Hitchin?" snorted Terry. "My fanny's itchin'! For fuck's sake."

"That's probably why she sticks to blow jobs," I said deadpan. That earned me a dirty look from Myfanwy and a slap on the back from the psychopathic rock star. He was still laughing when we reached the tour bus.

The inside was tidier than you'd imagine. Aside from a stack of VHS videos – including 'The Thrilla In Manilla', 'Debbie Does Dallas' and 'Metallica: Cliff 'Em All' – and a few scattered rock and porn mags, everything looked spic and span. In fact, the only things that looked even remotely out of place were the photos randomly sellotaped to the wall. Among the many polaroids of generously breasted groupies, whose AAA passes meant they had obliged at least one of the road crew with a blow job, there were also tasteful shots of very different birds. Mostly swallows. No obvious pun intended.

He followed my gaze. "A swallow, the wind's favourite toy. Do you know that quote?"

I shook my head. "Jules Renard."

"Don't know him, Tel."

"French geezer. Writer. I like it because it has a deeper meaning. The swallow thinks he's in charge but really the wind is the guv'nor. It's the same with us. We think we're running our lives but it's fate that has the real power. A twist of fate can change everything. So, it's good to be a little humble, even if you are cock of the walk and master of all you survey. Sure we should be cautious and plan well, but the big things are often out of our control."

Terry wasn't what I expected. Behind the rock star front, he was not only bright, he seemed deeper than most. Almost philosophical in fact.

Compared to most villains at least.

He gave me a hard, almost menacing look. "Why the fuck should I trust you, Harry Tyler?"

I wasn't fazed. "I dunno, Tel. Except I want nothing from ya and if you tell me to fuck off now, I'd be happy just to have met you and the boys. I'm not after nothing." I paused and added, "And I was taught to be cautious too."

He smiled. "How old's your mother?"

"937…and I can tie a bow like you wouldn't believe."

He grinned broadly, reached out his right hand and we exchanged masonic handshakes. (I wasn't on the square but I knew enough Old Bill who were to be able to bluff my way around it.)

"So, you're off to the States later this year, Plumstead was saying. How's that going to play?"

"That, Harry, is our boot in the door. Proper tour, proper fuck-off stadiums, tens of thousands of punters a night. The record company bought us onto it and that is precisely the only reason why any band should sign to a major. A lot of bands say the record companies rob you. I say let 'em, because we will rob them back five times as hard. A hip little indie like Small Wonder couldn't have done that. Rough Trade couldn't, Neat Records couldn't. Even Secret couldn't. They haven't got the clout."

"Well good luck with that." A thought occurred. "Has anyone ever tried to go into a record company as a long firm fraud? I'd imagine it'd be pretty easy to pull off."

"We never have, but Uncle Wilf did."

"Uncle Wilf?"

"Wilf Pine, family friend. He used to manage Sabbath. A few years ago, him and Charlie Kray started managing a rock band, built 'em up, got gigs and paid for cracking reviews. They started to get a lot of record company interest, all the A&R men were buzzing around, and after a while they signed a deal for a hundred grand advance. They banked it, transferred the money out of the country, and by the time the record company bods got on to them for product, they've broken up the band, their management company were kaput, they had a load of moody receipts from a recording studio, and no product because of a robbery that had been properly reported to the Filth and investigated by friends of theirs in the CID who to everyone's surprise cleared them of any involvement."

"Fucking great."

"It worked a treat. The band had no idea."

I knew about Wilf Pine. I'd heard his name a lot. As well as managing Black Sabbath, Uncle Wilf was the only Englishman ever to become a made man in the New York Gambino family.

"Of course, that kind of fraud only really works once in a generation," Terry continued. "The real racket is owning the record company itself, or at least being properly on board in one. Look at MCA and Sal Pisello in the States with the 'board of directors' – Rocco Musacchia and Gaetano Vastola."

"More uncles?"

"Ha, no. Friends of friends. Friends of Wilf's to be precise."

"It sounds daunting, the States. I don't mean the mob side, although those fuckers would terrify me. I mean opening for Metallica."

"No, we will piss it, Harry. We'll give their crowd exactly what they want – a show, hard, fast and skilful. We're already on heavy MTV rotation, the college radios have been playing us for years, Yank audiences love the Brits – and we're talking their language, freedom, opportunity, making your own luck. The next studio album has a track called 'We Are The Living' because the Septics also love a bit of Ayn Rand, and a ballad called 'Rosie' about our dearly departed late sister that is absolutely ideal for FM radio. It isn't so much an album as a business plan, and a perfect one – it ticks every box and it will take us to the next level. Then we'll whip out a live double album to chase the ace. Hold up, I need a gypsy's…"

I looked around quickly and found a handwritten A3 sheet under the magazines detailing dates, places and weights. Drugs probably. Careless but inconclusive. I noticed that there was a signed, framed picture of Margaret Thatcher standing proudly on the table.

"The only honest person to enter the Houses of Parliament since Guy Fawkes," said Terry, as he returned. "Though Enoch was all right. The fucking silly lefties hate Maggie, and rightly, because she tells it like it is. 'Pennies don't fall down from Heaven,' she said. 'They have to be earned here on earth'. Translated into the real world, that means encourage the risk-takers, keep taxes low and keep regulation light to give us grafters a reason to get out of bed in the morning. Maggie stands for people like us, Aitch, proper people trying to earn a few bob, not the layabouts and ponces."

I figured now was not the time to say I thought Harold Wilson and Sunny Jim Callaghan had been the best PMs of my lifetime. There's a lot to be said for free enterprise, of course. But it gets corrupted and bent out of shape. Too often private profits trump the needs of the people – from Peter Rachman to stock market rackets. We caught the Guinness Four, but how many did we miss?

I glanced around the bus and spotted a pile of dog-eared paperbacks ranging from 'Hazel' to 'The Tibetan Book Of The Dead'. In the middle of the stack was the almost inevitable 'The Profession Of Violence' – the only obvious link to the Bishops' other world.

"Didn't Maggie also say an honest day's work for an honest day's pay?" I said flatly, with no hint of sarcasm. "I had her down as law and order all the way."

He shrugged. "What's illegal now won't be forever. Sir Francis Drake was a privateer, a fucking pirate, now he's a national hero."

"He died of dysentery, didn't he?"

"Shit happens. We're honest grafters at the end of the day, Aitch, supplying a demand. The drugs trade is market capitalism in its purest form. If people didn't want to buy shit, we would be out of business. It's not like there are adverts for free-basing in the middle of Coronation Street."

I laughed. "Sniff it up with Gail Platt."

"Well, she's got the bugle for it."

"Imagine Hilda Ogden on crystal meth. She wouldn't need no curlers. Her barnet would curl up of its own accord."

"It's her Stanley who could've done with a morning livener. Work-shy Northern git."

I laughed naturally. No need to fake it.

"I get what you're saying, Tel. I wouldn't be surprised if puff wasn't decriminalised in our lifetime…"

"And Charlie and whizz. They were legal once and will be again and people like us will be seen as pioneers. But all I want to do is make a killing now and clear the fuck out before it's all above board and regulated and taxed to buggery."

He poured us both a large Macallan, killing the bottle. "To Maggie!"

"To Maggie."

I smiled broadly, largely at the absurdity of the prime minister's outsider radicalism being pressed into service as an unlikely intellectual justification for the carnivorous violence and feral psychosis that had powered Terry Bishop's life-long game plan.

He chopped out a fat line on a copy of the Financial Times and handed up a gold-encrusted sniffing tube with 'Hammer' artistically inscribed on the side. I obliged, feigning gratitude. I didn't mind a toot on duty for the sake of appearances – most of the villains I'd encountered had been bang on the gear. You just had to be careful not to let your mouth start running off on it.

"Charlie Richardson taught me about stocks and shares when I was a nipper," said Terry. "Me uncle Stevie knew him well."

"Stevie?"

"Steve Knight. Again, not an uncle but family and all male relatives were uncles back then."

"I didn't know you were close. He's proper legit now."

"Head screwed on. That's the way to do it. Of course, he didn't have a soppy cunt for a brother…"

I let the words hang in the air, thinking he'd open up. Instead, he took a huge snort and changed the subject. "The other great thing about the free market is you can buy the competition."

"Which is what you've done?"

"Since the start, mate. That's how it works. Turn rivals into partners. Junior partners, kicking up to us."

"Smart. But not that little Camberley mob, they're not playing ball? Not that it's my business…"

"Sometimes negotiations ain't enough, Harry. Sometimes you need to crack a few heads to teach the watching world a lesson. Like we did in Manchester. The Gypsy wankers will have to learn the hard way."

"Pour encourager les autres."

"Yeah, all of that. Here, want a spliff?"

He passed me a fat joint, pressed play on the cassette deck and the bus filled up with the sublime beauty of Miles Davis's 'Kind of Blue'.

"Now this is proper mellow…"

"I love it. Uncle Steve's favourite. John Coltrane is class too. I've been getting into him lately."

"You think about retiring, Tel?"

"Never. Even when I've got half a yard tucked away in the Caymans like Steve has, I'll still be making music."

I picked up Thatcher's photo.

"She won't last though," he said morosely. "Those posh cunts are a proper nest of vipers. Some of these back-stabbing Oxbridge toffs make Brutus look like a fucking girl guide."

"You think they'll knife her?"

"I don't doubt it. The Old Boys brigade wanted to take the reins back from the upstart." He paused. "Every great leader has enemies, Harry. Fact is, if you go to your grave without upsetting anyone it's a sure sign you've achieved absolutely fuck all in your life."

I hesitated, and then just said it, "You too, Terry? The enemies?"

"I'm looking over me shoulder all the time, Aitch. I have to. The minute you let your guard down, they'll strike. And it'll be some weasel you trusted, someone who you thought was on the firm. It might even be family. It'll be the Tories who do for Maggie, not the soppy lefties, you mark my words."

"She had that other quote didn't she, the cocks may crow but the hen lays the eggs?"

"Yeah, well, she weren't right about everything. We know that in the real world, her world as well as ours, the cocks are the ones on top doing the fucking and most hens are eternally grateful to be the fuckin' fuckees."

He reached into a cupboard and pulled out a fresh bottle of vintage Macallan single malt. "Look, Harry," he said. "This is the reason I asked you over here. I want you to take this as a thank you."

"But that's got to be worth five large…"

"And the rest. You stepped in and saved Wolf when there was nothing in it for you. It's my pleasure to give you a thank you gift. I will be offended if you don't take it."

***

Half an hour later, pleasantly buzzing I opened the tour bus door and saw five heavy looking, long-haired bikers lurking about in identical sleeveless black leather jackets directly in front of us. The backs of the jacket made it clear that they were 'Gypsy Rebels, Camberley'.

The fat one at the rear of the group, just four feet to our right, turned and saw us. He noticed Terry behind me at the same time as I clocked the Webley Top-Break revolver in his hand. There was no time to think, just to react. I swung the superior single malt bottle straight at his hairy head, knocking him sparko… while simultaneously bathing him in delightful vanilla and green apple aromas.

Too slow, fat boy.

As the others turned, I slashed the nearest one across his already scarred cheek, and then span around and kicked a third biker right in the orchestras. He crumpled like a cheap suit. But the fourth guy, the tallest and broadest of the lot, got his arm around my neck from behind. The fifth, a goblin-faced heavy swinging a bike chain, made straight for Terry Bishop who ran back into the tour bus and locked the door behind him. As I tried to break the tall guy's grip, the biker with the bleeding cheek punched me straight in the solar plexus. I felt my diaphragm spasm. This was getting serious. And painful. I kicked out hard, aiming at my new attacker's right knee, kicking it all the way in. As he fell, crying with agony, I rotated my body until I was looking straight into the taller man's warty face, stuck my right leg behind his legs and used my bodyweight to put him on his back. His head smashed against the tarmac and I finished him off with a head-butt that shattered his nose.

"That's it, twat." The fifth biker was pointing the Webley at me. I was fucked. Until the bullet from Terry Bishop's silenced revolver went right through his skull.

At that point the cavalry arrived. Chad, Jimmy "The Crank" Kossler, Plumstead, Spider, a snarling Psycho Manny and another one of the Iron Army firm who I didn't recognise came roaring out of the hotel back entrance with Stanley knives in their hands.

"You took your fuckin' time," snarled Bishop as he helped me to my feet.

"Boss, we never knew. It was only when Chad popped out for a puff that he saw it."

Terry half-smiled at the 6ft 5 black hooligan. "Thanks Chad. But fucking hell. If it weren't for Harry here I'd have been brown bread. That's both of us this man has saved now, me and Wolfy."

"Respect, Aitch," said Chad. "You took out four of the cunts on your Jack."

"Who was it? Camberley?" growled the narked-looking Psycho Manny.

"No, the Scottish fucking Widows. Of course it was Camberley you pillock, can't you fucking read? Where's that ugly cunt Mungo?"

"On the missing list, boss."

"You know what to do with these, Crank," said Terry. "This one..." – he prodded the first biker's comatose body – "this miserable fat fuck, got a £6K Macallan facial, so wake him up and light his kisser up like a Christmas pudding before you pop the cunt."

Terry turned to me. "You okay, Aitch?"

"Yeah, just a bit bruised, Tel."

He lowered his voice. "It's rare for me to be lost for words Mr Tyler but I genuinely can't thank you enough. If there's any favour I can ever do you, no matter how big, just ask."

"There is one small thing, Tel."

"Go on."

"Well, I say small but she looked a good six foot. Tasmin was her name... I think she can help heal my pain."

Terry Bishop laughed. "Miss Millington will be all yours, Harry. Stand on me."

As we walked back to the party, little Billy Fenwick came out of nowhere.

"Tel, it's Mungo, he's going loopy. You've gotta help."

We followed him at a trot to the other side of the hotel to see Mungo shaking Myfanwy Hitchin about like a rag doll in the jaws of an agitated guard dog. The woman begged him to stop but he slapped her hard. "You fucking shit-cunt slag," he shouted. "You fucking two bob whore..." Then he slammed her head hard against the brick wall and she hit the deck sparko.

He towered over her, looking properly off his nut. Myfanwy was out cold but he clearly hadn't finished with her. I'm no shrink, but the horrible bastard's mind was as mangled as a motorway pile-up.

We broke into a run. At that moment Wolf Bishop came tearing out from the hotel entrance, grabbed hold of Mungo and started to pull him away from the poor woman. They were maybe twenty feet ahead of us. Mungo span round and punched Wolf clean off his feet. And then he just hovered over him, poised and glaring, with his fist clenched. Until he noticed us.

"It ain't his business, Tel," he growled. "And it ain't yorn neither."

Terry Bishop spoke slowly; his words were heavy with menace.

"Don. Step away from my brother."

Mungo ignored him and went to stomp a steel-capped Doctor Marten boot down on Wolf's face. I ran straight at him and sent the big lug crashing down with a high shoulder tackle. But Mungo was back up like a jack-in-a-box and he caught me with a brutal right that had me staggering back like a midnight drunk.

Fuck me, that proper hurt.

I stepped back. He came back at me again and threw a roundhouse left that would have knocked me spark out if it had connected. I ducked back, leaning to my left, and felt it swing by, but lost my footing. I was down. Mungo loomed over me, building up for the go-for-broke knock-out blow. Luckily Terry Bishop got between us, and chinned him hard. It was a good punch and one that would have put many a man to sleep. But Mungo just seemed to soak it up.

"I said leave it, Don. Let. It. Be."

The larger man stopped and glared at me as I went over to Myfanwy. Mungo's unlucky victim was out cold, caked in her own claret. The big bastard took a step towards me.

"Don, I won't say this again," said Terry. "Fucking leave it."

The gun was back in Bishop's hand.

Warwick's face twisted into a picture of frustration and venom. He said nothing. He just turned and stomped off, kicking a dent in the door of a parked BMW for good measure. Chad made to follow.

"Let him go," commanded Terry. He turned to Billy. "You probably saved this girl's life, Bill. Listen, take this" – he pulled a roll of notes out of his pocket and pressed it into Fenwick's hand – "get her home, make sure she's okay, make sure she won't blab, give her this, and send her some flowers tomorrow morning from the band. If she seems damaged in any way, give Wungy a call and he'll get a quack over who won't ask questions. Chad, go with them please mate, just to be on the safe side.

"And Harry, once again thank you. Mate, if we was in the Kate Carney you'd get a Victoria Cross for what you've done here tonight."

He turned to Plumstead. "Mark, have you still got drop offs to do tonight?"

"Yeah, boss. Me and Mungo were supposed to be on our way about now."

"Crank here will go with you. You can drive, Jimmy, okay? Harry, can you ride shotgun? Or have you had enough? The three of yous should be enough."

I nodded. "No problem."

"Good man." He squeezed my shoulder. "You ain't coming up to Cov are you, so if I don't see you tomorrow, I'll see you at Stratford, yeah?"

"Wild horses couldn't keep me away."

"Cushty." Terry helped Wolf up from the tarmac – he looked concussed. Condition normal, I thought. Then he shook my hand in an unusual way.

I lent forward and whispered. "How old's yer mother?"

"733," he said with a chuckle, adding, "We'll discuss this further, bruv."

Then he pulled Wolf tightly towards him and moved off.

"See ya then."

"Yeah, laters."

***

Plumstead took me inside the roadcrew bus, to pick up copious supplies of class A narcotics.

"Here, Aitch, have a line."

I took his rolled-up fiver and sniffed. "Ta."

"We'll save the rest for Ron."

I grinned. Ron as in later-on.

"You know why they're called Class A drugs don't ya?"

He shook his head.

"Because when you snort 'em your instant reaction is to go 'class, eh?'"

"You plum."

He laughed. "'Ere, Aitch, have you seen this before?"

He showed me the infamous six-foot-long metal case known as 'The Coffin'. It was filled to capacity with baseball bats, pick-axe handles, coshes and heavy chains. The deadlier weapons were hidden in a secure compartment built into the wall where the drug supply was also kept. He took out a Glock 17 and gave me an S version Beretta – "a lovely little April", as he rightly said. April Fool = tool. Do try and keep up.

The Crank got in behind the wheel of black Transit van and we drove off to the first meet. There were only two to get through, both with representatives of different gangs who were based about ten miles apart. I stayed in the van as instructed, which was handy as I was surprised to recognise two of the guys at the second meet from the soap-dodgers' rave Pete Harrison had been revolted by earlier in the month. I sank in the front seat but luckily with our headlights on full beam the crusties hadn't clocked me at all.

Plumstead came back with an envelope stuffed with bullseyes. "Scruffy looking cunts," I said.

"Yeah," he replied. "But they're good earners, Aitch. You okay for another half-hour, mate? We've just got one more job to do."

"Sure."

We drove on to Clifton. Crank parked up in a deserted side road and he and Plumstead disappeared with night vision goggles, cameras and brand-new leather gloves. About twenty-five minutes later they came back in good spirits.

"Don't tell me, you were owl-spotting," I joked.

"Better than that, we just cased a joint near the downs."

"I thought you lot had moved on from the drumming?"

"We were just on a recce, mate. In and out without leaving a trace. Like the SAS. Or my micro-knob on a cold day."

"Hence the turtles. But how could you get close enough to the gaff for a good eyeball without the security code?"

"Easy when you've got someone on the inside."

"I won't ask." I paused as we moved off and added, "These drums must be worth about three mill."

"Yeah, he's got his arse in the marmalade, mate. But it's what's inside this one that makes it special."

I nodded. "We done now?"

"Yeah, Aitch. Back to the hotel mate."

"Got any cassettes in here, Crank?"

"Aerosmith, AC/DC, Rose Tattoo…"

"Stick on a bit of Rose Tattoo, will ya?"

He obliged, and they banged their heads along to 'One Of The Boys' while I discreetly looked out for road signs and landmarks.

***

The hotel bar was still open when we got back so I got a round in.

I had the draft lager.

"Any good?" asked Plumstead.

"No. It's shit mate. I'll be glad when I've had enough of it."

He and Crank laughed, but not for long.

"Last orders," said the barman.

"Bollocks."

"Want a scotch, Aitch?"

"No ta. I'd better get some kip."

I walked up to my lonely hotel room feeling a little sorry for myself. The adrenalin had long faded, and Mungo-inflicted damage was starting to hurt like hell. I opened the door and was surprised to find that I wasn't alone after all. I had a visitor and, as it happened, Tricia Hodges – Tasmin Millington's real name – was a hospital nurse. She got to work quickly on my bruises, using the mini-bar ice and then compressing the swelling with an elastic bandage from room service. Then she got to work on me.

In bed, I'm normally the one in charge. Not tonight. The lofty black South Londoner practically ripped off the rest of my clothes, then pinned me down and rode me hard. After we'd both come twice, she flipped me over and gave me the best massage I'd ever had. I was hard again in about fifteen minutes and she jumped on top of me for another go. Such stamina! I'm fit but she was seriously tough to keep up with.

After her fifth orgasm, Tasmin finally settled down beside me and we cuddled like proper lovers, revelling in the touch and the smell of our sweat.

Ten, maybe fifteen minutes later, I got up and fetched two brandies from the mini-bar. She looked at my face and tutted.

"Your lip, it's swollen."

"Yeah, it had a slight collision with Mungo's fist."

"That man's an animal."

She took an ice cube, wrapped it in a handkerchief and applied it to the swelling.

"So which job do you like best?" I asked.

"Nursing has its own rewards, Mr Tyler, but the non-medical work pays a damn sight better."

"There must be downsides, though; things that you hate about it."

"Of course there are. The fat old men with their wobbly bollocks. All that flab, all the halitosis..."

"At least you don't have to kiss 'em."

She pulled a face. "I never kiss a client. Never. But it does give me great pleasure when they want the dildo. I can work off my disgust by fucking them hard. Like a piston."

She giggled.

"Have you slept with many of Iron Hammer?"

"Just the brothers."

"Who was better?"

"Terry!" she answered immediately. "Wolfy's a bit... weird."

"How so? Is he into the dildo?"

"Oh yeah, he asks to be 'punishment fucked', he likes that a lot. But it's not just that. It's more...well, the first time we fucked, he got me on all fours – I thought he wanted it doggy style. But he went down on me from behind. But not on my minge. He started licking my arse."

"He did what?"

"He kissed and licked my arse."

"What?"

"He stuck his tongue up my arsehole."

"Why would he do that?"

"I dunno. It's a gay thing. Rimming they call it."

"Nah, I reckon he must have thought you were the first black pope and wanted to kiss your ring."

Tricia laughed.

"He likes being hurt," she said. "I had to beat him once. He asked me to treat him like, and I quote, 'a Jewish dominatrix with PMT punishing Hitler'…"

"Oh for fuck's sake."

"Whereas Terry is the other way. He likes to inflict pain. Not with me, I'm not into that, but if a girl is into masochism, he will hurt her."

"What's your fantasy, Trish? What turns you on?"

She looked at me and realised I was serious. "I like it standing up. We face each other, I've got my legs wrapped around my man and he puts his hands under my butt and lifts me up and down as he thrusts into me. I'm a dominatrix for a living as Tasmin, right, so I'm used to being in charge. But when I'm with someone I trust, someone I care about, I love them being in complete control of me. He has to be strong to do it. Mmm. I could come just thinking about it..."

"Let's do it."

"What, no."

"Come on, I can lift you."

"With those bruises? I'm black, you're blue."

"I can do it."

"K. Can you get hard again?"

"Already there..."

She came as soon as I entered her and twice more before I'd finished. Then we collapsed onto the bed and slept all night.

The alarm went off at 6.30am – it must have been set by the bastard who'd had the room the night before. Still, it gave us the chance for one more, slow, tender session. We both climaxed simultaneously and then she kissed me softly on the lips, just to show I wasn't a client.

"Come to breakfast," I said when she came out of the shower and started to get dressed.

"I can't. I have my other job today."

"Well, come to party on Saturday then?"

"As an escort?"

"No not as Tasmin. Come as Tricia. Come as a woman. Come as my date."

She kissed me again. "I might just do that."

I'll level with you. I really liked the bird and she banged like shit-house door. But I was using her. Having Tricia on my arm on Saturday was another way of me saying, I am so one of the gang that when I'm not saving your lives I'm schtupping your salts. I'm Harry Tyler and I'm one of your own.

***

Over a hotel full English breakfast, I gave Plumstead the full Tyler – boasting about our night of passion, elaborating the details and reliving the earlier fight with the bikers blow by blow.

"You wanna hang out this morning, Aitch?"

"Can't mate. Got some trades back in the Smoke that can't wait."

"Shame, me and Kenny are driving out on another couple of recces."

"Oh yeah? Where this time?"

He lowered his voice. "Same area, two other drums. But this time in daylight. We're posing as, what d'you call em?, twitchers."

"Three gaffs altogether? I thought you said it was just the one. You're back on the rob big time, son."

"No mate, this is definitely a one off – one job, three targets, all the same day, then scoot. The first geezer, the one last night, he's minted. Tel told me this morning he's the managing director of some lab off the A40."

My ears pricked up. "Benston?"

"Yeah. Terry tell you about it?"

"No. It was on the news. Some boffin there got a proper spanking the other day."

"Well, anyway the geezer's cake-o. He's got some painting Tel is after."

"Who by?"

"Not a clue. Some old French cunt."

I polished off my third cup of Rosy. That narrows the field to about five hundred artists then, I thought.

"Right," I said. "I'm off to graft. See you Saturday."

"You certainly will, mate."

We shook hands and he gave me a master mason's grip, which I returned. A penny dropped. If all the Bishop gang were on the square, it was odds-on that half of Stratford nick would be as well. It only takes a few to be on the take and the Bishops are bullet proof.

I pondered. Plumstead's real name was Mark Corrigan. We must have a senior bod up at Grand Lodge who could pull a few strings and find out who else is in Corrigan's lodge. At least one Bishop, I'd wager. Or maybe two, and a mob of local Plod. Like say Tony Wilson, the detective who conveniently went on the missing list the night that the shit went down in Canning Town...

I made a mental note to run this by Mark Nixson as soon as... Not all freemasons are bent of course; in fact, in my experience most of them are charitable souls. But like the job, it only takes a couple of bad apples to sour the whole damn orchard. Throw in some local councillors and a magistrate or two and that was all you needed for a culture of corrupt cronyism to fester.

The hotel hadn't had their newspapers delivered so I popped out to buy *The Times*, just in case I had a message. I spotted a paper shop over the road, next to a McDonald's and sauntered over. But what I saw through the restaurant window nearly stopped me in my tracks.

It was Terry Bishop and Tim Robb in a booth together. Bishop and Robb! How? Why? It made no sense.

I ducked back. They hadn't seen me. This was hugely unexpected and I had to take it in slowly. It looked like they were old mates, for one thing, which was odd. And it looked like they were both eating sausage egg McMuffins, which was odder still, since Comrade Tim was an ardent and outspoken veggie.

I bought *The Times* and waited in a shop doorway over the road, making out was reading it. Bishop left first, Robb a little later. Only now he was eating a quarter-pounder. He'd waited till 10.30 for the menu to change.

What the fuck were they doing together?

***

I called Mark Nixson from a phone box at Chippenham services and told him about it.

"Talk about the odd couple," he said. "I'd hadn't foreseen that."

"Nostradamus couldn't have foreseen that."

"What do you think that relationship is built on?"

"Drugs would be my guess. Robb is a dealer."

"Could it somehow be connected to the attacks?"

"I'm not sure how that would work. My best bet would be that they've got some kind of drug-dealing alliance with Robb as the junior partner. I mean, he could never take on a firm like the Bishops, even with his crusty rent-a-crowd in his pocket. They would wipe him off the map. Besides, the two of them seemed really friendly."

"It's certainly very odd. Is it a threat to our operation in any way?"

"Nah. Robb didn't spot me, guv; neither of 'em did. I'll just be extra cautious on Saturday, just in case he shows up."

"Okay, keep me informed."

"Oh guv, before I go, let me know if there are any art robberies in the Clifton area this week."

"Will do. Connected to this?"

"Yep. Corrigan and co have been on the prowl."

I hung up. The DI seemed happy, but I wasn't convinced that this was about drugs at all. Terry Bishop, Tim Robb. Together? There had to be a bigger picture. Something I was missing. But what? I wouldn't have had Robb down as a Mason.

Chapter Seven

Friday, May 25, 1990.

I hadn't been expecting to see any of the Bishop gang until tomorrow night's gig at Stratford Town Hall, so I was surprised to get a call from One-Gin inviting me down to the Coach & Horses – universally known as "that Jewish place", as in "the Kosher Horses" – tonight. Turned out that because tomorrow night was family night, with wives and mums on the after-party guest-list, Terry had decided to organise this "boys only" event which of course was nothing of the sort.

Tonight was more for the boys and their girlfriends – for the lads and their mistresses. Mark Corrigan's bit on the side was a surprisingly classy solicitor called Gemma. Wolfy wasn't married but came with his new flame, Vanessa, a woman he'd met in the Athena Apollo the night before the bikers' benefit gig. She was tall and fit with large dark eyes, long striking platinum blonde hair and striking Nordic cheekbones; throw in tight black leather trousers, a midriff-revealing black top with buttons down the front and a studded dog collar and this was a woman who once seen would never be forgotten. Except... as our eyes locked, I realised I knew her from somewhere and that she knew me from somewhere too. Yet I had no idea of when or where we'd met. And it was obvious that she had no intention of discussing it. Not in public at least.

"This the man who saved my life – twice," said Wolfy as he introduced us. "Harry this is Vanessa."

"Nessa to my friends," she said with a warm smile.

"Charmed," I said, shaking her hand. Neither of us acknowledged that flash of recollection, but I have to admit it unsettled me. When you're in my line of work you deal with a lot of people on a short-term basis and most of them are of criminal stock, so it's important to have a bloody good memory for faces. Now I'm not one to boast but I have got one of the best – I could have won everything on the Generation Game conveyor belt standing on me prick – yet here I was drawing a total blank. One wild card was bad enough; to work with two was plain reckless. If I could get Mark Nixson on the line, I knew that he would tell me to abort. But no. I had to front it out. Ooze confidence. Invincibility.

"Can I buy any of you a drink?" I asked, as casually as I could, keeping my smile warm and my eyes peeled. I needed to buy myself time to think.

"It's a free bar you plum," laughed Plumstead.

"We're good," said Wolf.

"I'll get meself one then."

I walked over to the bar with a casual swagger. Chad, who had a little blonde sort on his arm, parted a throng for me and patted me on the back. Where did I know Nessa from? Wherever it was I knew for sure that we hadn't fucked, and I was pretty certain I hadn't turned her over.

"Forsyte's please love," I said to the glum-faced middle-aged barmaid, tapping the Stella pump.

"There he is!" I felt a hand on my shoulder and turned to see a grinning Terry Bishop. "More on cue than a snooker ball. Good to see ya, son, I'd like you to meet my very good friend Janice Hancock."

I put my hand out and looked up only to realise he had Victoria Boosler on his arm.

Tim Robb's Victoria Boosler.

Wearing a dress that stuck to her as tightly as clingfilm.

What?

"Jan, this is Harry Tyler. He's a good'un."

Vicky Boosler, here? With Terry? Posing as Janice? What the fuck was going on tonight? I was confused as hell but again I hid it well.

"Charmed," I said, holding out my hand to shake hers. She ignored it and pecked me on the cheek.

"Nice to meet ya, Harry," she said in an accent that had wandered a very long way from her usual Surrey tones. Less Guildford High Street, more Romford Market.

In any other line of work, I'd think I was being set up by Beadle's About. But this was a lot more serious, and distinctly unnerving. Now there was not one but two birds who shouldn't be here. One of them could sink me like the Belgrano. The other was still an unknown quantity. I had no choice except to brazen it out.

"You too Janice. I'm no expert on linguistics but you sound a bit Essex to me, am I wrong?"

"Ho! Bang on! He's right on the button," laughed Terry, patting my back. "Who needs Henry Higgins when you've got Harry Tyler?"

"That's a good strong name," said Janice. "Do you do any tiling?"

"He does a bit of banging, or so I've heard! He likes laying pipe…"

"Oi! Can I point out that I'm the only one here who's come on his Tod!" I said, with mock indignation, adding, "I think I might have to try me luck with Doris behind the jump. Everyone else here is spoken for."

"Ho, he fancies a bit of grumpy-pumpy," said Terry with a chuckle.

"Whatever floats your boat, darlin'," said Janice-not-Vicky.

"She'd fucking torpedo mine," replied Terry with a grin.

"What am I today, the Human Sponge?"

"Maybe 'Doris' will squeeze you dry," joked Janice.

Terry laughed and held up his hand. "Listen, I need to have a word with Wolf about tomorrow. Can I leave Jan in your hands for a bit, Aitch? So, you can fight off any of the hounds that will inevitably come sniffing around her?"

"It would be a pleasure."

"Great, back in a bit."

As he left, Janice leaned into me and said, "I'm nipping out for a fag, come with." An order, already.

I followed her trying to look happy-go-lucky. This was a riddle wrapped up in a mystery inside a pain in the arse. Bad enough that Terry Bishop had some kind of nefarious relationship with Tim Robb on the go. But now Robb's equally suspect *unterleutnant*, Vicky Boosler, was hanging off his arm calling herself Janice…

The fact that she hadn't blurted out my other identity suggested that she had something to hide too. But what? And was the unknown quantity that was Nessa anything to do with it?

Outside, I downed half the pint of Stella in one gulp.

"What's going on, Vicky?"

"Stick with Janice," she hissed, adding "I was going to ask you that very same question."

"Ho! It's Harry boy!"

I waved at One-Gin as he waltzed up with a glamorous black woman and gave him the thumbs up.

"Aitch, this is Jade."

"Wotcha Jade."

"See ya inside, mate."

"We need to talk," Janice said urgently in her more familiar accent. "But this isn't the place. Terry has put me up at the Tower Hotel for a couple of nights – do you know it?"

"By Tower Bridge, St Katharine's Dock."

"The very same. Meet me there tomorrow, we need to talk."

I nodded.

"9am."

"Okay."

"And say nothing to anyone here."

"No problem." It was pretty obvious that Victoria had as much to lose by being caught out here as I did. Which was a relief. But if Terry was mates with Tim, what the fuck was she up to?

A few of the gang spilled out, lager-handed, talking about the Buster Douglas and Evander Holyfield fight that was still a few months away – the smart money was on Holyfield.

"So why this place?" said the woman I had to call Janice as she looked the pub up and down.

"Rock history. One of the early venues Iron Maiden used to play."

"And they're bigger, right?"

"Yeah, but don't let this lot hear you say that. In their book, they're the only band that matter."

"You're looking good… Harry." The smile was coquettish. I felt a twinge. She sure knew how to play me. I felt awkward. Then the cavalry arrived.

"How's it hanging, Aitch?" said One-Gin with a lager in one hand and Jade in the other.

"All good, mate. You know Janice?"

He nodded. Course he did. Jade leant in for a kiss on the cheek.

"No Mungo tonight then?"

"No mate, he's cried off. Some family business, he said. Too embarrassed to show his big ugly boat, we reckon. But he's running the security squad all day tomorrow, so his beautiful kisser will be fully on display."

"Are you expecting trouble?" asked Janice.

"What, on our manor? Leave it out, Jan. These are our streets. But it never hurts to be careful."

He shot me a quick but unmissable glance which I took rightly to mean as "don't mention Camberley".

Terry and Wolf emerged so I ducked back into the bar. I wouldn't stay here long. There was no telling who else might bowl up. A good evening of beer, banter and complimentary seafood had lost its appeal thanks to two mystery birds, one of whom seemed a lot more dangerous than the other.

Besides, I reasoned, because of that, more than ever, I would need a clear head tomorrow.

I plotted up with the rest of the band and road manager Vic Galanis on a corner table. There was some small talk about the Hammers, and then we got around to music. Punk was my era, The Jam in particular, but I could talk 70s rock all night long. Their girlfriends were something else. Butch Halfwit was married to a Danish model called Mia, Sid Silverton was slipping her sister Ena the goldfish, while Frarny Bydewell was engaged to his childhood sweetheart Gillian who worked at Billingsgate Market and did a bit of stand-up comedy on the side.

All the women looked bored stiff as we droned on about the glory days of Thin Lizzy, Uriah Heep, Atomic Rooster and Third World War. Working Class Man!

"You're lucky Henry Gibson isn't here," Butch told Mia. "I'm not saying he's dull but Henry's monologues on Henry Cow could send a speeding Mod to sleep in two minutes flat."

"I never liked them," Vic said emphatically. "Tuneless posh boys."

Vic, who didn't look too well, then told us about his early years driving for the Small Faces – "a proper band".

"Can I shake your hand please Vic?" said Butch.

"Sure, but why?"

He held it out and shook it vigorously.

"Just so I can say I've shaken the hand of a man who has shaken the hand of a man whose fingers have been up Chrissie Shrimpton."

"You are gross!" said Gillian.

"Sorry Gill. But come on, Chrissie Shrimpton!"

"You know 'Talk To You' was written about her?" said Vic. "I knew her sister Jean too."

"You knew The Shrimp?"

"That's what Vic's wife calls his cock," joked Gill, giving a throaty cackle.

"Now, now, Gillian," he replied. "You wouldn't want it on the end of your nose for a wart."

"Gentlemen," I said. "Finally we have reached my level."

I smiled but my mind was in turmoil. I'd just caught Terry glancing over at me with One-Gin. Neither of them looked happy. Something wasn't right. Bishop. Robb. Boosler. I couldn't work it out. I needed to get away and think it through. I must have missed some clues, something that would make sense of this mess. I felt my heartbeat quicken. I was just about ready to make my excuses and leave – citing the lure of the massage parlour next door to the Athena Apollo – when someone started to play footsie with me. I didn't think it was Butch either. I looked up and caught Ena's eye. Now I didn't see that coming.

Nor did I anticipate a tap on the shoulder from One-Gin.

"Can I see you for a minute, Aitch? Quiet word. In the khazi?"

"We know what yer doin'!" cackled Gillian.

I wasn't so sure. A crafty line at best. But if Vicky had blabbed, I could be bang in trouble. I slipped my right hand into my pocket to touch the cosh, just to make sure it was there. It was, firm and hard. I ran my fingers over it and felt reassured. Charlie or carnage, which way was it going to be? I was ready for either.

In the event it was neither.

"It's a bit delicate, Harry," he said. He didn't seem angry, which was a relief. Just worried.

"What's up?"

"It's the boss. He, uh, he's got a dose."

"He's what?"

"He's caught the clap, we're not sure who off. But the point is, he obviously don't want Sylvie to know, and he wants to keep it from Janice too. So we're going to come up with a reason he's got to leave early and he asks if you'd take Jan back to the old Gasthof. Can you do that for us?"

"Sure I can," I said, only slightly concerned.

"He also asks if she can come with you tomorrow like she's your plus one at the after party, so she don't look like a spare dyke at a rugby club wedding."

"Well yeah, but I was coming with Tricia, you know, Tasmin."

"Don't worry. I'll let Tas know. She'll understand. And you'll be doing Tel two giant favours, which won't be forgotten."

"No problem."

It was, I suppose, an offer I couldn't refuse.

***

We sat silently in the back of the sleek black limo that One-Gin had ordered for us. I went to say something, but Janice-Victoria shook her head and nodded slightly towards the driver. Good point. Like walls, Aloysius Parker had ears...and there was I with my own Lady Penelope.

I looked out the window at the curling edges of Stratford. Milady seemed a bit tipsy so my plan was to drop her off at the hotel reception and scoot back here to that massage parlour next door to the Athena to give the night a happy ending.

That didn't happen.

A couple of minutes later I felt Victoria's hand at the top of my thigh. It lingered there a while. I looked back at her and felt her fingers slide towards my cock which rapidly hardened, straining the fabric of my Farah slacks. A solitary fingernail glided slowly along the length of it. I was now as hard as quickset cement.

I moved in to kiss her and she responded, softly at first and then harder and more urgently as her tongue probed deep into my mouth. I cupped her right breast and her hand start to rub me. How I didn't come there and then was anybody's guess. Her fingers moved to my zip just as we pulled up outside of the hotel.

"How much do I owe you mate?" I asked the driver.

"Wungy said it's on the firm, chief," he replied.

Of course, the Bishops owned the car hire firm. Let's hope the driver didn't clock us playing tonsil tennis in the rear-view mirror and report back.

I took out a Jacks and then changed my mind and slung him a cockle instead, just to be on the safe side. It probably paid to keep him sweet.

I got out, pulling my jacket down to hide the obvious, and opened the door for Janice.

"Why thank you, kind sir."

"I'll see you safely in and head off then, madam."

"Don't be so rude," she said in her best Vicky accent. "And don't be so fucking plebian. Do not be scared of me, Mr Harry-Peter. I won't bite, unless you want me to…"

We walked across the lobby to the hotel lift. A family got in before the door shut and we moved to the back of the elevator where she deliberately pushed back against my undiminished erection and wriggled. It took a lot of self-control not to groan.

Inside her room, she pushed me onto the bed, pulled off my strides and boxers, hiked up her skirt and straddled me. "Unfinished business," she murmured.

Vicky pulled her underwear to one side and took me deep inside of her. At that moment I was really grateful that she was on top. If I'd been in the driving seat it would have all been over at the first thrust after all of that build-up.

Victoria set the pace above me, going at it like a jackhammer, as I recited the names of the Scotland football team in my head. This delaying technique worked effectively, unless you tried it with England teams, because as soon as you reached the goalie it was all over.

That's Seaman, if you're wondering – an old joke, yes, but it always tickled me.

I knew she was coming because what began as a long low moan erupted into a high-pitched screech loud enough to wake the dead. Strewth. I never had her down as a screamer. Memo to me: next time earplugs.

I flipped her over and tried to take my time but images of Ena and Tasmin and then Vanessa flooded my mind unbidden and I reached me vinegar with a groan followed by an unseemly giggle.

"Well, that was worth waiting for," Vicky smiled. I rolled over and she peeled out of her clothes as I got shot of mine. We lay naked under the sheets, snuggling like lovers for all of five minutes before the inevitable interrogation began.

"So, should I call you Harry or Pete?"

"Harry is my real name," I said truthfully.

"So why Peter?"

I sighed. "I had upset some proper nasty bastards in South London. Mates of the Arif family, if you've heard of them. I had to get out of the Smoke. And as these particular bastards have a lot of friends, I decided to move out Bristol way, to the fucking wild west."

"And you changed your name…"

"As a precaution. I also changed me hairstyle and the clothes I wore." There was enough reality in that for me to sound doubly convincing.

"Animal rights?"

"I genuinely hate animal cruelty. I can't see a fox hunter without wanting to chin the cunt. I'd done stuff with the Hunt Sabs years ago, so it made sense. And it was exciting but not in the way my dealings with a bit of villainy were. I hooked up with the Bishops by accident and as they view South London as their deadliest enemies, I figured I was safe enough to come back to the East End as me."

She thought for a moment, taking it in. My story had the ring of truth. I pushed my advantage.

"What I want to know is how posh well-spoken Victoria from Surrey ended up pretending to be an Essex girl called Janice."

"A bit of subterfuge on my own part," she said. "I knew Timmy had something going on with Terry Bishop and wasn't sure how such a relationship could possibly work without him getting seriously hurt. So, I decided to check him out. Hence Janice."

"Risky," I said raising a quizzical eyebrow.

"Not really. I was careful. I approached them via their record company as a freelance journalist and requested an interview with Terry for the Stratford Gazette to tie in with the big town hall gig. The interview went well. He obviously fancied the pants off me."

"Obviously…"

"The Gazette were keen to run the exclusive and, after my glowing piece ran, he got straight back in touch."

"So, you're a recent item."

"Yes, very. And as yet an unconsummated one. My plan was just to hang around long enough to find out what Terry Bishop is up to with Tim Robb."

"Talk about an odd couple…"

"I was worried Tim was getting something that was way out his depth and potentially life-threatening. What would a brick-hard East End gangster have to do with a privately educated animal rights activist?"

"That's the $64 million dollar question."

"It's certainly one that needs answering. On the surface their relationship is at best peculiar and, at worst, extremely worrying."

I nodded. Victoria's explanation was on the same level as mine – superficially convincing even if, on closer inspection, it would probably turn out to be full of more holes than a barrow full of Swiss cheese at a Wild West firing range.

"You've got nice eyes," I said.

"You've got a nice cock," she replied.

"Thank you."

"I want to know what it tastes like…"

We took it slower the second time.

***

I slept lightly and, at around 2.30am, when Janice was snoring gently, I got up for a Jimmy, carefully scooped up her handbag and took it into the khazi. Inside I found a Deringer, a couple of grams of cocaine, an Ultra Compact Pearlcorder L400 Micro tape recorder, a slim covert camera, a high-quality listening device, and my cosh – when the hell did she half-inch that? There was also a perfect ID for Janice Elizabeth Hancock. If this was fake, it was an expert job. But drugs and tape recorder aside, none of this fitted her cover story.

At 4.44am I heard Victoria get up. She made a similar trip; she picked up my wallet from the bedside cabinet and took it into the bathroom with her. Hmm.

She came back and turned on the bedside light. I made out that she had woken me up and opened my eyes with a groan. She had the Deringer pointing straight at me.

"Okay, now Harry or Peter, tell me who the fuck you really are."

I yawned. "I took the bullets out of that thing hours ago." I sat up in bed and shook my head. "And to think I thought you liked me…"

I knew I could have her nicked for cocaine possession and a firearms offence, so I took a gamble.

"Who are you working for, Vicky?"

"What?"

"I know you're not Old Bill, so who are you with? That ID you've got is a work of art. You don't get that from the Hunt Sabs."

She hesitated. I pushed my hunch.

"You work for Box, don't you? It's okay, I've signed the Official Secrets Act too."

"You're… U/C?"

"I am. And you're?"

"You're right. Box."

"Embedded with Tim Robb because of the escalating violence, I'd guess. So, presumable you're genuinely here to check out the nature of the links between Robb and organised crime."

She sat down on the bed. "Yes. Are you coming at it from the other direction?"

"Not quite. I infiltrated Robb's mob first and got pulled out after the Bishops killed one of our guys. Seeing Timmy and Terry together came as a complete shock, especially when they were getting on like a loss-making business on fire. Before then I didn't have the slightest inkling that the two jobs could be connected."

"Tim is playing it close to his chest but he has dropped hints that he's been buying Semtex from a London supplier, who I'd presume is Terry Bishop."

"That would make sense, but it doesn't explain why they'd meet in person. Terry likes to keep well away from anything dirty these days. So there has to be something more…"

I paused. "Any idea why the Iron Army would have been staking out three millionaire mansions on the same day that the two of them met for breakfast?"

"Not yet. But I do know something big is about to go down. I have to be back down there as Vicky by pretty early tomorrow morning because early next week is when it, whatever 'it' is, is due to kick off."

"And why this? Why us?"

"When I saw you in the Coach & Horses, I just assumed that Terry Bishop must have sent you to infiltrate Tim's barmy army as the underworld equivalent of a sleeper agent, to keep an eye on him and report back."

"And there was me thinking it was my boyish good looks…"

"That as well. You are, what's the expression? As fit as a butcher's dog."

"You're not bad yourself, for a girl."

I took the Derringer from her hand and shook my head, playing hurt.

"You were going to shoot me."

"I'd have winged you. And then I'd have kissed it better…"

She leaned in for a kiss. Seconds out, round three.

***

We had room service breakfast and believe me I was glad that I'd ordered a full English. Victoria had drained me. We ate in bed, on silver trays.

"So," I said eventually. "How did you become a spook?"

"It's quite a familiar story."

"Not to me. I'm intrigued."

"I was fresh out of Cambridge with a first in Classics," she shrugged.

"Ancient Greeks and Romans, and all that jazz."

"That's about it, the jazz being literature, philosophy, culture, language, architecture…" She smiled and teased the end of a sausage with her tongue. "And I thought I'd follow daddy into the Foreign Office. Instead, I found myself being interviewed for months on end in different unmarked government buildings and answering a barrage of questions – did I believe in god, and if so which god; did I vote Tory or secretly sympathise with the Militant Tendency; where did I stand on ethics – don't do the obvious lisp joke!

"Did I like dicks or fannies or any combination of the same…I have to admit I had an inclination at this point that this wasn't a standard FO vetting. Then they asked me to sign the Official Secrets Act and levelled with me. I was a few months in when I was invited to a day with other candidates. We did role play, exercises, written tests and yet more interviews. I must have done well because a little later I got driven to Slough House for another intense grilling from senior people including a Harley Street shrink. Then they asked to speak to my parents, some old friends, some friends of friends…it was a long process of background checks, basically, and digging for dirt – if you dropped acid at school or sucked off the headmaster they needed to know. And at the end I passed. I was a spook, with certified clearance to the highest level."

"Is that when you got the James Bond kit?"

"Nothing so glamorous. Firstly, Bond was MI6, and secondly, we don't even get – what would Harry Tyler call it? – decent 'wedge'. The money is shit. No one does it for the wages. You're serving your country. The job is the reward."

"And at that point what happens next?"

"I was posted to F Branch, which is counter-subversion – Commies, Reds, fascists, terror sympathisers, anarchists, left-wing nutcases, right-wing nutcases, religious nutcases, animal 'liberationists' and so on."

"Enter comrade Tim."

She nodded. "Yup. It's my first big job. My first infiltration. Up until now, I'd been on surveillance jobs, planting bugs or working with the team to intercept communications."

"How are you finding it?"

"A breeze, to be honest. In my experience, most fanatics are desperate to find other people who share their mindset, or weak-willed people who they can win over. Like a lot of egomaniacs, Tim Robb is quite needy. He has to be the big fish in his little pool with his admiring congregation of cranks."

"And I suppose it didn't hurt that you must be the best-looking woman he'd ever met."

"I'll take that compliment without complaint. But it's a relief that as Janice I can finally wear some decent clothes and proper make-up instead of slumming around looking like a rug-munching troll. How about you, Harry, why do you do it? Why did you become a cop?"

I thought for a moment. "I suppose I just don't like seeing the weak and powerless get abused by the strong. The only Bully I ever liked was on Bullseye."

The Jim Bowen joke soared way over her head.

"Have you been doing this long, the infiltration side?"

I did the sums. "Coming up for four years in the field now," I said finally. "And almost exactly four years since Harry Dean passed out as a UC operative at the tender age of twenty-seven after four months of hard training. Before that I'd spent six years in uniform, followed by a transfer to the CID and then the Essex wing of the Regional Crime Squad. I didn't hang about..."

It all seemed so long ago. I told Vicky how, as Harry Tyler, I'd started working at Ron Claven's scrapyard in Charlton, and how I'd moved from there to working with Ron's pals Potman and Noodles over in Southall before coming up against the Nixon family for the first time. The stories spilt out of me, like a geyser of oil shooting out from a freshly struck vein in an old black and white comedy Western flick.

I caught myself. "Sorry, Vic, I don't normally rabbit on like this. It's just such a rare opportunity to have someone outside of my gaffer who, a) I can talk to about this shit, and b) who will actually understand what it all meant."

"Don't apologise. It's fascinating."

"There's plenty more..."

"And plenty of time for you to tell me. We will do this again, won't we?"

"You try and stop me."

Her hand found my thigh. "Once more?"

"With feeling..."

***

It was still pretty early, 9.15am, when I came out of the shower, but I couldn't stick around. There was a lot going down today and I had to have a debrief. I felt her eyes linger as I towelled myself down.

"What's the plan?" I asked, as I pulled my Iron Hammer t-shirt over my head and straightened it out. "Shall I pick you up, at around 5.30, and we grab a quick bite at the Tai Pan before the gig?"

"Sounds good. What have you got to do earlier?"

"Check in, and then head down to the soundcheck at the town hall at about 3pm. Good to show me face."

She nodded. "Harry, have your boys got any bugs in place at the moment?" she asked.

"We have now. The phones at all of the Bishops' businesses."

"Waste of time," she said crisply.

"Why?"

"The only place they ever talk proper business is in the upstairs office at the Athena Apollo," she said. "Terry has it swept by bent Old Bill every couple of months."

"He told you this?"

"Your friend Plumstead did. He's a bit of a blabbermouth, isn't he?"

"Had he had a few?"

"Hasn't he always?"

"Very handy. Thanks. And so you're cool for tonight?"

"I'm hot for tonight," she said with a wicked glint in her eye. "But yes, come here and we'll go together. I'm going to head into town and pick up something to wear."

"Odds on you'll get the same thing or better for half the price down the Roman Road."

"Yes, but Terry's paying and he told me not to spare the expense. Who am I to disobey orders?"

I laughed and popped back into the bathroom for a quick Gypsy's. When I came back out, she was on the phone. She held a finger to her lips and I nodded.

"Hi Tim, it's Vicky... are you missing me? Good. Listen doll, I know I said I'd be back tomorrow but I've been having such fun with my sister that I thought I'd stay for the weekend and come home late morning on Monday. Is that okay? ... oh really? ... uh-huh, uh-huh, tomorrow? ... in that case forget it, I'll come back now and you can fill me in... no, I have no idea, he never said... okay, I'll start packing now... yes, I should be with you by 1pm, 1.30 at the latest... love you."

She put the phone down and looked at me.

"Whatever Tim is planning, it's been brought forward; it's happening tomorrow now."

"Shit."

"Isn't it just? I'll go back straight away and keep on top of it. He asked after Pete. I said I had no idea when you'd be back."

This was tough. I was in so deep with the Bishops that to leave now would jeopardise everything.

"I'll check with my guv'nor, but my gut says that if you're watching Tim, I'd be better off keeping an eye on Terry."

"Yes, makes sense. Listen, Harry, also tell him that your boys don't need to be involved in Bristol. We'll handle Robb, we've got the manpower."

"What will you tell Terry?"

"I'll think of something. He'll be at the Athena. I'll ring him there. And of course, as last night didn't happen you wouldn't have known anything about the domestic crisis that has sent me packing. You just saw me safely to the hotel room, like a gentleman."

"Of course. Okay, that makes sense."

I bent down and kissed her gently on the lips.

"Until the next time."

"Oh, don't worry Mr Tyler, I'm very much looking forward to the next time..."

Chapter Eight

Deptford

I had a mid-morning meet with Mark Nixson at the Mangal Café, a little Turkish dive I knew on Deptford High Street – the wrong side of the drink, and far too deep into Millwall territory for any of the Bishop firm to be floating about. Nixson's team had stuck me in a safe house in Limehouse, part of the Old East End that was in the process of being rapidly yuppified, although I'd only been in it long enough to dump my clothes and park the car outside. From the hotel, I had to grab a cab to get back there to pick up my Granada from outside the gaff; consequently, I arrived in beautiful downtown SE8 a few minutes late.

Like many a Deptford good time girl, the caff had seen better days. What was left of the paintwork was fading and its once welcoming façade had been stripped of colour over time. But again, like many a mature local woman, there were still plenty of pleasures to be had on the inside. The smell of the sucuk – Turkish sausage – made me wish I'd skipped the hotel nose-bag.

DI Nixson was already tucking into the "kahvalti special", a veritable feast of eggs, sausage, kasseri cheese, bell peppers, tomatoes and scallion doused in oregano, with simit, a Turkish bagel, on the side.

The owner Sadi caught my eye and smiled broadly. "Aitch, it's bin too long mate," he said in broad Cockney. I shook his hand.

"Good to see ya, Sid."

"What can I get ya, son?"

"Just kahwati coffee for now please mate." I nodded at Mark's roll. "And some fig jam for my pal's simit."

"On it like a car bonnet."

I quickly brought Mark Nixson up to speed as he made notes. We paused as Sadi delivered my coffee and the DI's jam, and then Mark lowered his voice.

"So, let me get this straight," he said in little more than a whisper. "There's something big going down in the West Country tomorrow which may or may not involve the Bishops, something that could involve Semtex 10 plastic explosives. On top of that, MI5 have had an operative we didn't know about imbedded with Tim Robb all the time you were there and the Bishops are caught up in a nasty drug supply turf war with an outlaw motorcycle gang from the mean streets of Surrey?"

"That's about the size of it, guv. But can you do me a favour and check out Victoria Boosler's status as quickly as you can, please? I need you to get Box to confirm that she is who she says she is. Just to put my mind at rest. Everything about her and her story seems legit."

"Of course. And no doubt she will ask her handler to do the very same thing about you. You don't know the nature of the relationship between Robb and Terry Bishop yet then?"

"No. Nor does our friendly neighbourhood MI5 operative. It's a bit of a puzzle. The pair of them seemed to be very friendly, close even – something which was confirmed by Boosler. But if this is just an arms deal, I can't get me nut around why Bishop is personally involved. He has been keeping criminal activity at an arm's length for quite a long time now; why put himself in jeopardy?"

Nixson thought for a moment. "It suggests that there's more to their relationship than we know," he said.

I resisted the temptation to channel Basil Fawlty and ask if his specialist subject was the bleedin' obvious. The DI paused. "Hmm. Anything else?"

"Just that the Bishops seem to have something pretty big going on in Bristol too, because they had a team casing some plush high-end properties down there. That could well be for another time but I don't like coincidences. The gang do seem to be fraying and falling apart at the moment. There's bad feeling simmering. Don Warwick wasn't there at the pub last night. Relations between the brothers are clearly pretty strained too. Terry doesn't seem to have much time for Wolf and vice versa. On at least one occasion I heard him refer to him as an 'AIDS-ridden faggot'."

"Pleasant."

"There are also rumours that Wolf wants out and is trying to sign a solo deal."

Nixson nodded and made more spidery notes.

"And guv, forget tapping their business phones. You need to have listening devices planted in the office at the Athena Apollo. That's the only place Bishop openly discusses business other than a golf course and consequently the only place there is a chance of him ever mentioning the names of corrupt officers."

"They don't own the Apollo, do they?"

"No, that's the beauty of it. Misdirection again. You'd expect Terry to do his plotting in a Manor House portacabin wouldn't you?"

Nixson grunted and made more notes.

"Did you see the pictures from Mark Brennan's funeral in today's papers?" he asked finally.

"No, I haven't had time to look at any yet."

"We were all there," he said with a touch of pride.

"I wish I had been," I said with genuine feeling. "The Bishops will probably have the pictures from that on their backstage dartboard tonight."

"A backstage dartboard?"

"They have a match before every game they play."

He shook his head and tutted. "We will get the arrogant murdering bastards, Harry. We owe that to Mark Brennan and his family... and to Catherine O'Mara and her unborn child... and all of their other victims too."

I nodded. "What do you want me to do about Robb, guv? Boosler will be back down in Bristol in a couple of hours. She says that Robb has been asking after Pete, but she also reckons Box should handle him on their Jack, and that we should butt out."

"Does she, indeed. What are the Bishops doing after tonight?"

"Not much, in theory. It's the end of the UK tour. They've got the next album to master – something big and brash for the Yank market because they're off on their big stadium tour there in Autumn – and if that happens, they will never look back. Before that, in the next week or so, Terry is planning to go to Minorca with Sylvie for a break, and Wolf is scooting off to Marrakesh with the new bird. But I'd be very surprised if they don't have something significant done about this Camberley biker gang, the Gypsy Rebels, while they're out of the country. Terry won't leave a sore like that festering for too long."

Nixson thought for a moment. "Well, you stick with them tonight Harry, and try to work out the missing links. I'll speak to top brass about Bristol. Local Old Bill will need to be on high alert whatever Box say. Whether we leave it all to the spooks or get directly involved is a decision above my pay grade. But we have got a dog in the race."

"Ha. Just don't call me Lassie."

"You not eating?"

"Nah, guv. Breakfast was on MI5."

"Well at least we got something out of them."

I smiled. If only he knew.

**

My safe house – actually quite a posh flat – was in Narrow Street, E1. It wasn't as narrow as it once was, but the street was the oldest part of Limehouse. The Grapes, which was just over the road from me, first opened nearly 500 years ago. Sir Walter

Raleigh set sail from there on his third voyage to the New World. You wouldn't think it now, but Limehouse was once the centre of world trade. To this day you'll find a lot of buildings there dating from the 18th century.

I got back, washed and changed into a fresh Ralph Lauren polo shirt, and some stonewash jeans. The Grapes served proper grub in their small upstairs restaurant but there were two other decent looking boozers in spitting distance – the old-school The House They Left Behind, literally a converted end of terrace house that had been left standing after the rest of the street had been demolished; and Booty's Riverside Bar was more likely to attract local duckers and divers. They also did a mean chilli, which took my fancy.

I ordered a pint of Nigerian lager and a large bowl of it, extra hot, then looked around for somewhere to sit. That was when I noticed Shirley Kelly up at the window looking out over the Thames. In profile she was a very handsome woman. Shirley spotted me, flashed me a surprised smile and started walking over just as a strong hand clasped my shoulder from behind.

"Harry." I knew at once that the sonorous growl belonged to Don Warwick. Could he have trailed me to Deptford? Had he guessed? If he knew anything at all it would compromise the job. And he'd be a hard man to nick. Or kill. I turned and kept my tone breezy.

"Mungo?"

He looked dishevelled.

"The same. What are you doing 'ere?"

"I've just moved in over the road mate. More to the point what are you doing here? It's a bit off the manor."

I was relieved to see Shirley's rear walking past us. She made for the door and didn't look back. Smart woman. She would have recognised Warwick from the mug shots. There can't be two people in East London who were uglier than 'Chucky' after an acid rain face-wash.

Mungo leant in closer to me – so close I had to stop myself wincing at the whiff of his halitosis – and muttered, "I needed to clear me swede, mate. Tel's been doing me in."

He looked at me. "Sorry about Swindon. I was hammered. No offence meant."

"None taken. Why this place, Don?"

"I used to come in here for a quiet one after dropping Wolf up at The White Swan, a little poof boozer up on Commercial Road he liked to hang out in. I'd plot up in here and he'd ring Ron behind the jump when he wanted picking up or chauffeuring somewhere."

"I didn't realise he was that blatant about it. I mean I'd heard the rumours."

"He's getting worse, mate. He don't realise how much the News Of The Screws would pay for a picture of a top rock star snogging an ice cream in a gay bar. It's right on their doorstep too. It drives Tel absolutely Garrity."

"Each to his own I guess."

"I don't mind shirt-lifters, but this is different, this could nause up the band and the business," he said, adding under his breath "the wrong kind of irons."

"Good point. So his new bird, is she a beard?"

His forehead crumpled. "No, he's shafting her an' all, greedy little cunt… Here, Harry, you want to buy a couple of grams for a ton?"

"I can't mate, all of my money is tied up in cash."

Mungo gave me a quizzical look and started to make an unsettling noise, a bit like a van trying to start on a cold winter's day. He was laughing.

"You're all right, Harry. You'll do for me."

"You keeping away today then mate?"

"Nah, I've cleared me canister now. It's the big one tonight, Harry. Home turf. I'll be there doing security. In fact, I'll head off for the soundcheck once I've had this."

He indicated a glass of neat whisky, which he promptly downed.

"I'll see ya down there."

"Yeah, laters."

I watched the big man lumber out of the bar. A ticking time-bomb primed to go off. Still, on the plus side that was the most civil he had ever been to me. Things were improving.

***

I turned up at Stratford Town Hall to see Terry on stage blowing smoke rings. He gave me a wave, and with his fag in his mouth, he sat on the edge of the stage with his precious Fender Strat and delivered a note perfect rendition of Eddie Van Halen's 'Eruption' guitar solo – which, I'm told, is incredibly hard to play.

I was enjoying it so much that I nearly missed the excitement.

Tipped off by Plumstead at front of house, Mungo and Jimmy The Crank pelted out of the Town Hall entrance in time to see two jeering men jump into a battered black Ford Capri. The fruits of their handiwork were plain to see: the letters MFC and LKI – short respectively for Millwall Football Club and Lions Kill Irons – spray-painted across the front of the building.

"Fucking no-good fucking Millwall cunts," snarled Mungo. He looked at Plumstead. "Give us the keys to your Fiesta," he commanded.

"Want me to come with?"

"Nah, there's only two of the cunts. Me and Crank can handle them. You lot get that shit scrubbed off the wall before the Billies turn up. And if any photographers show up before you finish, fuck 'em off."

It was the last time I saw Mungo alive.

***

Don 'Mungo' Warwick followed the Capri at a reckless speed along Stratford Broadway and into the high street, throwing a left at the Bromley-by-Bow roundabout to take the A12 to the A102 and towards the Blackwall Tunnel. They were at the traffic lights north of the tunnel when he caught up. He got out of the Fiesta to check that he'd got the right black Capri. It was two cars ahead with a Millwall scarf stuck across the back window. Got 'em! He started forward but the lights changed. Mungo dashed straight back and tailed them through the pipe.

The Capri turned left into the car park of the Mitre Arms, just south of the tunnel. Mungo had been there before for a comedy night where they'd ripped the piss out of Helen Lederer. The Tunnel Club, they called it. Well there was nothing funny about the pain he was about to inflict on these two Millwall mugs.

The big man got out of his car, swinging a crook-lock in his right hand. Jimmy The Crank was right by his side with a Stanley knife ready to go to work. The fucking idiots were still sitting inside their motor. Probably tossing each other off, he thought and grinned. Too late he heard the footsteps behind him. A billy club knocked the Crank straight out and another lashed across Mungo's back. He roared, turned and took out his first attacker with one mighty swing of the crook-lock, knocking out his oppo with a hard, straight left. But eight more Millwall came from nowhere and formed a circle around him. All of them were tooled up and they came at him at once from every direction.

Mungo wasn't a slouch on the cobbles – he had been street-fighting since St Joseph's primary school. He knew exactly what to do. There was a skip to his right, so he KO-ed the one ginger geezer who was blocking his way to it and pulled out a two-foot length of scaffolding pole. That evened the odds a little.

CRACK! He clocked one of the bastards right around the canister, sending him straight to the deck, and then pulled back the pole and took out another whose legs seemed to crumple under him in slow motion.

One on one Don Warwick would have dropped them all.

But there were just too many of them. One of his attackers whacked his right arm with a baseball bat and he dropped his tool. His arm hurt like fuck.

Mungo booted baseball bat guy in the bollocks and chinned another with a good left. They were definitely more scared of him than he was of them, and that helped. But although he got in some solid punches, a baseball bat to his knees brought the big man down and a series of blows from coshes, hammers and truncheons did the rest.

Don 'Mungo' Warwick, the Iron Army's answer to Lenny McLean, was out cold.

It was only then that the two men got out of the Ford Capri. The passenger, Jacko Roberts, felt the weight of the World War One single action Colt in the inside pocket of his combat jacket as he walked across to where Warwick's unconscious body lay on the tarmac and barked the simple order "Turn 'im over". His crew obliged and, on his order, they dragged the still unconscious Crank over and laid him out next to the bigger man. Roberts picked up the discard length of scaffolding pole and smashed in the Fiesta's windscreen.

The four Millwall who were still standing formed a loose semicircle around the bodies, shielding Jacko from the busy road. He then pulled out the six-shooter and fired three rounds point blank into Mungo's chest. The big man's Combat 84 t-shirt slowly turned red. Jacko stood over The Crank and fired another three into him.

Game over.

Satisfied, he handed the driver, Lars Oxley, his Stanley knife and said "You know what to do".

Later that night, when he re-played the two callous murders in his head minute by minute, Jacko Roberts realised he had an erection. He let his right hand slide down his body to cradle it and came immediately.

***

Back in East London, the band finished the soundcheck with an impromptu romp through UFO's 'Doctor'.

"All right, Aitch? How did that sound?" asked Terry Bishop as he jogged down from the stage.

"Proper out of tune," I replied.

He laughed. "Everyone's a fucking rock critic."

"No, it was terrific, Tel. You should do this for a living."

We were joined by One-Gin, Plumstead and Chad. Wolfy barely gave us a second look. He just walked off arm-in-arm with haughty Vanessa and her perfect cheekbones.

"Has the bird turned up from *Kerrang!*?" asked Terry.

"Not yet boss," said Plumstead.

"Well if she don't show soon she can do it over the dog."

"They on side?" I asked.

"*Kerrang!*? Yeah. They love us. But this is just some little feature about my favourite guitarists. I might mess with her head and throw in Ernie Isley and Steve Lukather."

He paused and looked around.

"Where's Mungo?" he asked.

"Not back yet boss," said Plumstead.

One-Gin explained why Warwick and The Crank had left the building. Bishop laughed. "I feel sorry for South London. There won't be any Millwall scum left alive. Oh, Wungy, I had Janice on the blower before I got down here. She can't get here tonight. A big family drama or some such shit."

"That's a shame," said One-Gin.

"No, mate, it's a fucking relief. It's one less thing to worry about with Sylv hanging around. It means you won't have to pretend you're shafting her, Aitch."

I smiled. "The very idea."

"Oh shit," said One-Gin. "I was supposed to cancel Tasmin for you Aitch and I completely forgot."

"Well that's a good thing, you berk," laughed Terry. "It means Aitch has still got a date for tonight and won't have to jerk off into the taramasalata at the end of the night like Mungo will."

"A beautiful image, Tel," I said. "Remind me not to eat any of it. You never know with that shit. It's fishy, creamy, salty…I reckon the old bubbles at the Athena toss off into every batch."

"I'm going to tell Panny you said that, they'll be after your bollocks with the chopping knives."

"That's if Tasmin ain't drained them down to teeny tiny currants," added One-Gin.

With their laughter ringing in my ears, I took my leave and headed back to Limehouse to get set for the night. At the flat I rang Tasmin and arranged to meet her for an early pre-show meal. Same plan as before, different bird.

***

The gig was sensational. The town hall was small – the capacity was only 150, but there were at least 250 squeezed in and nobody seemed to care. Palms had been greased, and the Iron Army were running the security. This was Iron Hammer's thank you to their most loyal, hardcore supporters. Economically it made little sense because they could have filled the place five nights running. Strewth, they could have sold out the Royal Albert Hall twice. But money wasn't the point (although plenty was made on the sales of pills and powder); the point was to give the fans something special.

If the coming US tour and album had the expected effects on Iron Hammer's status, then this loyal crowd would never get a chance to see the band up close and personal like this ever again.

I plotted up at the back with Tasmin, who kept slowly grinding her shapely arse into my crotch "because of the crush". It had the desired effect.

There was no denying the band's energy or the storm of electricity they generated on stage. Iron Hammer strutted around like cocksure cartoon pirates, goading the captive crowd into paroxysms of delight. Heads banged, shoulders shook, and the horde of hard rock fans almost pogoed in ecstasy – there was nowhere for them to go except up.

"Are you ready to rock?" hollered Wolfie. "YEAH!" roared the crowd. "We can't hear ya!" shouted Terry. "YEAAHHH!" "Come on East London, you can do better than that!" "YEAAAHHHHH!" "That's more fuckin' like it."

Two hundred and fifty fists punched the air and kept on punching. From 'Iron Hammer' to 'Fort Vallance' via 'Biffo' and 'Love Bumps', the audience of hardcore fans were eating out of the band's hands. They were rewarded with exploding firebombs, old B-sides like 'Cayote Kate', an extended 'Dalston Devil' and a brand new number, 'Vampire Lover', played live for the first time with Wolfy bouncing around the stage like Tyson and an elongated guitar solo that seemed to soar up and kiss the very edge of heaven.

The first encore was inevitable. Then they left the stage. For a couple of minutes, the air was thick with chants of "More! More! More!" Eventually Terry Bishop walked back playing with something that sounded new. It started with chopping chords as hard as paving stones, but when the rest of the band were in place, it sped up into a Cockney terrace singalong of 'Maybe It's Because I'm A Londoner'. At the first chorus they were joined by a line of eight glamorous high-kicking precisely co-ordinated dancing girls, sporting feathers. The women could have wandered in from the Palladium. They were identically dressed in microskirts which showed off the whole of their legs and there wasn't a man in the audience who wasn't glued to every one of their synchronised kicks.

As a spectacle, it was incredible.

Tasmin was so excited that, while the audience drifted out to receive a complimentary tub of jellied eels, she dragged me into the ladies and made me shag her standing up in one of the cubicles. This unexpected joy had the added bonus of meaning we missed the final tape of the Cockney Rejects singing 'I'm Forever Blowing Bubbles' playing over the PA.

***

There was a fleet of limos laid on to chauffeur the firm back to the official after-show party at the Athena Apollo, but we decided to walk; it was no distance.

At the restaurant we were greeted by Terry's wife Sylvia dressed in black shorts, sheer tights and a sparkling top hat. She was stunning. Angelic, almost. How much did she know about her husband's nefarious activities, I wondered? Probably not that much. He'd keep the worst of it from her, that was for sure.

Tasmin pointed out various famous bods scattered around the do, including a former Iron Maiden guitarist, the bassist from the now defunct Cockney Rejects, a couple of up-and-coming boxers, three ex-West Ham players and four well-known Page 3 girls.

I soaked up the atmosphere, noting the number of people wiping their noses as they emerged from the bogs. Charlie was obviously here, as were significant older underworld faces from Hackney and Islington, along with the Knights who I wouldn't have had down as heavy metal fans.

These older, heavyweight villains were in a private corner, sealed off from the rest of the party. Other hardcases in attendance included notorious hooligans from Poplar and Mile End as well as an ICF contingent. Five of the befeathered dancing girls were here too, huddled together near the stairs, waiting to be shown up to the office by an over-eager Panny.

The tallest one, a blonde, caught my eye. I winked and she smiled back, but she looked understandably nervous to be in such company.

How much were the Bishops splashing out on this, I wondered? The free bar alone must be setting them back £40k, probably more. There were waitresses walking around with champagne, and over by the front window was a lavish buffet occupying a twenty-foot table that included lobster, steak, rotisserie chickens, whole salmon, the obligatory jellied eels and tray after tray of Coquilles St Jacques.

'Scarred For Life' by Rose Tattoo was pounding over the sound system when I caught my first glimpse of Terry. He didn't look happy. He came straight up to me and asked anxiously if I'd seen Wolfy.

"Not yet. Not since I saw him on stage."

"It's a bit of a worry. Him and Vanessa said they'd walk here, but that was an hour ago."

"Maybe they stopped for a kneetrembler," said Tasmin.

"Yeah," I said. "He could be reliving his youth by slipping her the goldfish in a bus shelter."

Terry smiled. "He could be. But with all that's been going down with Camberley, I'm fretting a bit. Mungo and Jimmy are still missing too. Are you up for a recce if Wolf doesn't show by midnight?"

"Of course."

"Good. The cabaret is due to start then, so no one will notice us ducking out. I'll get a little posse together."

He called out to Wungy. "Come and have a quick word please, mate."

Wungy changed direction, stopping only to give me the large vodka and tonic he was carrying. "I was just taking this to the Profit," he said. "Can you deliver please Aitch, she's on her Tod."

I looked at Tasmin for guidance. "The Profit?"

"Terry's mum. She's hovering about over there by the buffet." I noticed an old woman with wild unkempt hair eyeing up the scallops and walked over with the drink. Her skin was so pale it was virtually translucent.

"Mrs Bishop? This is from Wungy. A large VAT."

She grabbed my elbow and stared at me intently. He eyes were as wide and wild as her hair was.

"I like you. Good auras," she said. "What's your name, son?"

"Harry, Mrs B. Harry Tyler."

"A good English name. Too many fucking foreigners around for my liking." She sniffed. "Even here."

"Terry's a bit tied up, Mrs Bishop. Can I take you to anyone? The Knights are over in the corner."

"Oh please do, boy. Just point them out to me. I can't think straight with this rotten music playing."

***

At 11.58, with the posse lingering over by the kitchen ready to make a discreet exit, Terry Bishop faked a smile and sauntered onto the improvised stage to the left of the bar. He signalled for the music to be cut, and, clutching a microphone, briefly thanked everyone for coming.

"Ladies and gentlemen," he said. "A nice round of applause please for our road manager Vic Galanis who is retiring tonight!"

Vic stood up and took a bow to a barrage of hearty cheers. "Vic has been with us since the beginning and we will miss him very much. Have a happy retirement my friend."

Vic raised his glass. "Come on, give him a proper East London send-off!" At that the crowd whistled and hollered and stamped their feet, until even Vic looked embarrassed by the fuss.

He sat down and when the applause faded, Terry went on, "Right, this is the moment you have all been waiting for my

124

friends. Please put your hands together for our very special guest, the legendary East End comedian Mr Jimmy Jones!"

The plan was for Jones to do fifteen minutes, followed by Jimmy Fagg and then a short blues set by Dennis Stratton and his band. That would give us midnight ramblers plenty of time to locate Wolf and put Terry's mind at rest, or so we'd thought.

As Terry introduced Jones, the crowd cheered so loudly that I nearly missed the sound of the front right window smashing. Someone had lobbed a brick in, showering the deluxe surf and turf buffet below with shards of glass.

"Kinnell," exclaimed Jones. "And I thought it was me who was bricking it tonight."

Essex villain Big Kenny Shaw was straight through the front door, his fist clenched into a ball of iron, but all he found on the pavement was Gary Lammin, the security guy, groaning in pain at his feet. The brick chucker had scarpered into the night.

The brick itself and the handwritten message attached to it were quickly passed to Terry. It was a ransom note that said simply: 'We have Wolf Bishop. We want £100,000 in cash, delivered personally by Terry Bishop. Call this number to make arrangements. If we don't hear from you by midday tomorrow Wolf loses his first finger'. The note was unsigned.

Seething with rage, Terry assembled a party of us in the Athena's upstairs office, which meant escorting the dancing girls out of it. "We won't be long," I told the tall blonde who I'd exchanged a wink and a smile with earlier.

"We'll plot up in the ladies, darlin'," she replied in broad Cockney. It was bravado though. I could see her hand was trembling.

In the surprisingly snazzy office, there was me, Terry, One-Gin, Chad, Plumstead, Spider and Psycho Manny, still looking about as happy as a scorpion with a cob on.

"So what do we do, boss?" asked One-Gin.

"We pay of course," replied Terry. "I'll phone this number tomorrow morning. Then we'll work out how to get Wolf and the money back and grind these gutless scumbags into the dust. I will take great pleasure in nailing these cocksuckers to the floor and slowing dripping sulphuric acid into each of their eyes."

I didn't doubt that he meant that literally, or that every word was being recorded thanks to Victoria's tip. If I knew Mark Nixson, the restaurant would have had a "routine visit" from their alarm company within twenty-four hours of me passing on the intel. This office was more bugged up than Jeff Goldblum in 'The Fly'. Any evidence gathered might not be legally admissible in court but that didn't matter. The intel could be crucial. It could be life or death. And if that meant my life, thank fuck for that.

"Who do you think is behind it?" growled Chad.

"Camberley, probably," said Terry,

"Or Millwall," said Plumstead. "The Roi Boys, the same firm who graffitied the Town Hall today."

"Nah, this is out of their league," I ventured.

"Unless Millwall and Camberley are working together."

"More likely Camberley have paid the little mugs to do their dirty work to escape retaliation," I said.

Terry nodded. "Now that's a good point. That sounds extremely likely but we'll know for sure tomorrow."

"Does this mean the other thing is off for tomorrow night then?" asked One-Gin.

"No, that is still very much on," said Terry in a voice as steely and assured as Margaret Thatcher addressing the nation during the Falklands crisis. "It just means we'll have to split into two teams – an away team and a home one. I'll have to stay here. Wungy, you head the away team with Plumstead and Spider. That should be enough."

"Where do you want me, Terry?" I asked.

"By my side, Aitch, if that's okay with you."

"Sweet. It's an honour."

"Thank you. I appreciate that, Harry."

I came down and saw Tasmin patiently waiting by the bar sipping a Manhattan. The party had started to break up the moment the brick had been thrown. There were just the stragglers left now. The tall blonde dancer was between us; she was on her own and still looking roughly as happy as a nudist in a nettle patch.

"You okay...," I paused for her to tell me her name.

"Jenny. Yes, thanks. I'm just waiting for my cab. The first one wouldn't take all five of us."

"I'm Harry, if I can help just ask."

"Thank you."

Just as I got to Tasmin, Tony 'The Geezer' Beezer showed up. He was an unliked 'plastic gangster' from Shepherd's Bush who had sold his largely fictional crime memoirs to a major publisher and pocketed a small fortune from the film rights. Terry Bishop took one look at the man in his camel hair coat with his bling-blitzed fingers wrapped around a fat cigar and knocked the smile off his face with a lightning-fast right hook.

"What was that for?" gasped Beezer from the deck.

"One, you weren't invited, two, cunts who write books are grasses, three, you're a fake and four, I don't fucking like ya. Will that do?"

"Sorry Terry, no offence."

Beezer staggered to his feet, dabbing his bleeding nose with a handkerchief, Terry turned to the doorman who was sitting at a table looking sorry for himself.

"How did that happen, Gary?"

"I honestly don't know, guv."

"Why were you on your Jack?"

"Billy had nipped in for a slash."

"He'd what?"

Knowing he'd dropped his friend in it, Lammin replied quickly. "All I remember is this little sort walked past me in boots and a red miniskirt, and the next thing I know some cunt has hit me smack in the kisser with a pepper spray. By the time

I could open me eyes whoever the fuck it was, weren't there. They was long gone."

"You soppy cunt," said Terry. "Your job was to be alert, on the lookout for trouble, not to go sniffing after some fuckin' gash."

"Sorry, Terry. But those legs…"

"Leave it."

"They were so long."

"I fuckin' told you…"

Terry went to punch him. I caught a glimpse of Jenny ten feet away looking even more distraught. Sylvie grabbed her husband's hand. "Not now," she said quietly. "He's been through enough. We all have." Lowering her voice to a soothing whisper, she went on, "I understand you're worried darling, but now isn't the time to make decisions. Let's get home. Let's plan it properly."

Terry turned to the watching firm. "See, she always knows what to say, this one. Lovely Sylvie, Sylvia my love. Either she's an angel or I'm pussy-whipped." He smiled broadly; his rage dissipated. "We'll meet back here tomorrow, 10.30am sharp. Okay?"

***

Outside, I waited with Tasmin for a limo.

"Are you coming back to mine?" I asked.

"Do you mind if I don't? Not tonight. I feel a bit shaken up after all that."

"Not at all, no problem. I totally understand." Sounded fine, felt gutted.

"There will be other nights, hon."

"Of course there will, darling."

Two limos pulled up simultaneously. I walked her to the first one, opened the back door for her and kissed her gently on the cheek.

"Laters."

"Yeah. Thanks Harry."

And that was how for the first time in living memory that I had ever gone to a party full of fanny and come away sucking me thumb.

As I sat in the back of my luxury limo, on me Tod, I mentally tossed a coin, and what do you know, it came down tails. We'd only got three yards down the road too.

"Stop the car please mate," I said. "I'll be two ticks."

I ran back to the Athena where Jenny was still waiting. Her mascara had run and she had clearly been crying.

"Jen, I didn't want to leave you here. You looked so upset. Where do you live? I've got a car outside. I can drop you off."

"I'm in Leman Street, Wapping, off the Highway. Are you sure? I don't want to put you out."

"No problem, I'm in Narrow Street. I'll just ask the driver to take you on. It's only about a mile further on to Leman Street. Probably less."

"Thank you, so much."

She gave me a squeeze and kissed my cheek. I could have grilled toast on the warmth of her relief.

***

She was pleased driving away. It had been easy. She had taken the big lug down, hurled the brick and dashed back to her Volkswagen Beetle in under a minute. Fifty seconds, maybe. Certainly no longer. If the other doorman had been there it would have complicated matters, but hey, perhaps fortune really did favour the brave. Sandra put her foot down and headed for the Blackwall Tunnel. At this time of night, she'd be back in Chislehurst by twenty past twelve. Job done.

***

Any lingering anxiety that Jenny might have had dissipated by the time the limo hit the Stratford one-way system.

"Thank you so much for this, Harry," she said. I noticed her voice was a bit throaty. A smoker.

"It's really no problem. I'll bung the driver. He'll be sweet."

"Weren't you with that pretty black girl?"

"Tasmin? No, she's just a friend. I'm a free agent" – well, yes and no, but in Harry Tyler's world you have to tell a few porkies when a top-quality leg-over is on the cards. "Shame you girls didn't get to dance, I was looking forward to that."

"What was the brick all about? I've never seen Mr Bishop so angry."

"Just business rivalry. Someone out of their depth. All shit, wind and piss. Nothing to worry about."

I paused. "How long have you been dancing then?"

Jenny proceeded to tell me a mini version of her life story while I smiled and nodded in all the right places.

I'm good at reading people – I have to be, my life depends on it; it's what I do. Jennifer Evison was basically a sweet girl from a hardworking Bethnal Green family who somehow had ended up on the fringes of very real danger. Fate can cut you that kind of deal sometimes. Especially if you're naive, as she was, lacking in street sus, and bereft of any kind of life plan.

I was especially good at reading women. I could generally call it right. And I knew instinctively that I had called it right with Jenny. The friendliness, the small touches, the twinkle in her eye, the physical tells...they all added up. If I called it on, my money said she'd spend the night.

"This is me," I said as the car purred to a halt outside Booty's.

"Oh, what a shame they're shut. I could do with a drink after all that."

See – her suggestion, not mine.

"I've got a bottle of plonk on chill in the flat if you like, and some beers. Oh, and a supermarket pizza. You're welcome to come up and I'll get you a sherbet home whenever you've had enough. If you like…"

"Oh I like. Thanks Harry."

The driver opened my door and I slipped him a score. She seemed even taller out here than she had looked in the restaurant, certainly taller than me in her heels and absolutely stunning in the moonlight.

I never needed to call her a cab.

***

I had set the alarm the previous morning so it would go off early enough to stroll up to Commercial Road to pick up the Sunday papers. I like to leaf through them over a bacon butty and a mug of Rosy, starting with the football and working backwards. But I wasn't alone when I woke up and the papers could wait. Jenny groaned.

"An alarm? Really?"

"Sorry doll, I've got to work this morning."

"What time?"

"I have to be back at the Athena for 10.15, Plumstead's picking me up at 10."

"So, when do you have to get out of bed?"

"9am at the latest, to be safe. It's ten past eight now."

Jenny smiled, put her head under the covers and started a long journey of kisses from my neck down. By the time she reached her destination, I was more than ready for what came next.

I repaid the favour and, in the process, rose to the occasion again. Jenny had come for the second time when my other alarm broke the silence. I looked at the clock. 9.10am. Now I had precisely forty-five minutes to get ready, grab some toast, drop Jenny off and get back here for Plumstead. The roads would be clear and at least parking near the Athena should be easy on a Sunday.

I got her phone number outside her flat, reluctantly declined her offer to "just pop in for a coffee", and then drove up to the garage where I filled up, bought the papers and flung them onto the backseat. I got back to the flat to find Plumstead pacing about outside.

"You're early."

"Yeah, slight change of plans. Tel wants in there a little earlier for a planning meeting."

He indicated a red Mini.

"Where's your Fiesta?"

"No fucking idea. I'm still waiting for Mungo to bring it back."

"So, this is the wife's motor?"

"Yeah."

"It suits you."

"Cunt."

***

Panny Adamos had laid on coffee and croissants for the meeting in the Athena's upstairs office. There were seven of us in total, including Terry, but you could tell nobody was feeling particularly magnificent. More like the Malignant Seven. They'd had a party up here the night before but Panny had been busy with the Vim. The only clue was a used condom he'd missed on the window ledge. We all saw it, but none of us remarked on it. It wasn't that kind of day.

Wungy produced a suitcase full of weapons from the band's tour coffin and invited us all to pick a tool or two. Then Terry gave us a prep talk about hitting back at our enemies ten times harder than they'd hit us.

"This isn't about good and bad, right and wrong," he said. "The only thing that matters is who is weak and who is strong." He paused, adding "And what are we?"

"Strong," we replied as one.

"What are we?"

"STRONG!"

"You're not wrong."

At 11am, he made the phone call.

"It's Terry Bishop," he said evenly.

"Good," a heavily distorted voice replied. "Mr Bishop, here is what is going to happen. I am going to give you an address. Write it down, memorise it, and then destroy it. You are to come to this address at 10am tomorrow morning. You will come alone on your motorbike and you will leave a bag containing £100,000 in used notes of mixed denominations behind the hedge of the property. You will then stand well clear while the bag is collected and the contents are checked. If everything is in order your brother Wolf will be released unharmed. If you try and arrive earlier or if you come with anyone else, our deal will be terminated and you will be scraping the remains of your brother's corpse up from the lawn instead. Do you understand?"

"Yes. But…"

"Say nothing more. The address is the Old Forge, Manor Park, BR7 5QI. Have you got that?"

"Yes."

"Do we have a deal?"

"Yes."

"Thank you. Your approach will be monitored."

The phone went dead. The look on Terry's face could have frozen larva.

"That's a Chislehurst postcode," said Plumstead. "A lot of wrong'uns in Chislehurst. A lot of Millwall, too."

We looked at Terry, who was lost in thought. For a while he tapped a pen against his thigh. But then he spoke very quickly.

"Gentlemen, we have a great deal to do in the next thirty-five hours. Wungy, you pick up the cash for me from the other place. Plumstead, I'm giving you a field commission. Until Mungo shows up, you are in charge of hitting back at Millwall and Camberley. Get a little team together. I want it done now. Start with Millwall this morning and we'll hit the fucking mild ones tonight."

Plumstead turned to me. "Fancy coming south of the river, Aitch? It's your manor too."

"No problem."

"Okay, me, you and Chad should be enough. We can..."

The office phone rang. Terry answered it and listened, his features darkening. After a minute he put the phone down without a word.

"That was our man at Stratford nick," he said, his voice thick with emotion. "The bodies of Don Warwick and Jimmy Kossler have been found in the carpark of a Greenwich pub – the one just south of the pipe. They had been mutilated almost beyond recognition. Both of them had been beaten and then shot three times in the chest at close range. The bodies were then stripped and urinated on. Across their foreheads the letters L-K-I and M-F-C had been carved, along with the letters R-B for Roi's Boys."

The air grew thick with furious swearing.

He looked up. "Don't get angry, boys. I don't want none of you to lose their cool. Suppress the rage. Use it. We are going to run this like we're the fucking SAS. Plumstead, get to the Bramcote, pick up anyone who looks like they might have been part of that little mob and get me the name of the piece of shit who shot our lads and desecrated their bodies. Then you find the cunt and you bring him straight to me at the Walthamstow place. You need to do this by 5pm to give you enough time to get down to Bristol for the fireworks. Can you manage that?"

Plumstead nodded seriously. "Wilco," he replied.

"Fuckin' wilco! Thank you wing commander. Now skedaddle and get the fuck to work, I've got plans to make."

Outside the restaurant, Plumstead looked worried.

"What's up?"

"Nothing, it's just… Chad, can we take your car mate? I mean we can't go scouting for Millwall in Her Indoors's little red Mini. We'd look a fucking laughing stock."

Me and Chad didn't stop giggling until we were on the A102.

***

The Bramcote Arms in Bermondsey sits near the confluence of two of South London's forgotten rivers – the Earl's Sluice and the River Peck. The pub was used as a watering hole by the cast of the police drama Dempsey & Makepeace and even featured in one of the episodes which was called, ironically enough, 'Mantrap'.

It didn't take long for Plumstead and his big wad of cash to find three thirsty friends eager to share his convivial company. He kept it light and kept the beers and laughs coming while he weighed up the other drinkers. It was easier still to identify the hardcore Millwall lads. They were plotted up in a corner and, after a couple of pints, helpfully burst into a snatch of a newly minted terrace anthem:

'He is 'ard, 'e's a fighter, 'e killed Mungo in the Mitre, with a knife and a bottle and a dose of lead, ICF will end up dead.'

Plumstead started to get up but stopped himself. Terry's words, "suppress the rage, use it", rattled around his skull until he managed to calm down and fake a smile.

"Who are these songbirds?" he asked his new pals.

"Bushwhackers."

"And a couple of them are Roi's Boys. They come in every week after Sunday morning football."

"Good lads," said Plumstead affably. "Listen, anyone in here do a bit of gear? I need to stock up for tonight."

"Yeah, one of them, Ray Pearce – the ice cream in the Last Resort T shirt. Shall I call him over?"

Bingo!

Plumstead nodded. "Please mate. But keep it discreet, obviously."

"There are no grasses in here, mate. Raymond!"

As it happened Ray Pearce dealt in Charlie, Es, puff, whizz, acid and pretty much anything else you needed to get you off your nut.

"I'll have one of Charlie and a pick and mix bag of the rest," said Plumstead. "Make it a ton's worth. I expect these boys will be having a bit before we finish."

His new friends grinned.

"No problem."

Ray nipped out to his transit van to pick up the goodies. Plumstead followed him to the door and gave Chad the nod.

By the time Ray Pearce came round, he was tied up in the back of Chad's car with the black man clutching a switchblade and leering at him.

They were parked in a cemetery. The Albin? Or Nunhead? Ray couldn't tell.

"Don't worry, Raymond," said Plumstead. "Nothing will happen to you, my friend. We just near a word with the fella you and your boys were singing about. Jacko Roberts, according to the second verse. He owes us some dough. Where can we find him?"

"I don't grass."

Chad plunged the switchblade into the fleshy part of Pearce's right thigh and twisted it. He screamed in agony.

"Keep it down, son," said Chad. "You'll wake the fuckin' ghosts… Here, Aitch, look at that claret. I don't think that there's a Tampax in the world big enough for a cunt this size."

Plumstead leaned in. "Now listen, Raymond. We don't want to make you bleed any more than we have to, because it's a hell of a job to get blood off of a fabric backseat and Chad here is a lazy cunt and he won't like cleaning it. But I do have to warn you that my dear friend is notoriously clumsy and if you don't cough quickly you might find that the next time he plunges you he might miss the thighs and go straight down the middle, d'you follow me? Instant circumcision… if you're lucky. Unhappy eunuch if you're not? Know what I mean? Now, where can we find Jacko Roberts?"

Pearce looked away from Plumstead and back at Chad who had pulled out the knife and was holding it hovering menacingly over his crotch.

"He'll either be in the Lord Northbrook or the Tiger's Head," he said reluctantly.

Plumstead nodded. "Lee Green. Good. I know it well. Old Tiger's Head or New?"

"Old."

"Height? Hair colour?"

"6' 3", ginger."

"See that wasn't so hard, was it?"

Chad opened the door nearest to Pearce, dragged him out and threw him headfirst at a gravestone. He was out like a light.

"Did you see what that tombstone said?" I asked as we drove off.

"No."

"It said, 'Not dead, only sleeping'. Who the fuck do they think they're fooling?"

Chad laughed. "So maybe ghosts are fuckin' sleepwalkers."

"Here we go with the voodoo shit!" I whooped.

Chad laughed. "Racist cunt."

"Pearce was lucky to be left just sleeping," muttered Plumstead. He looked round as we stopped at a set of traffic lights.

"Raymond would have made a good voodoo doll, very easy to stab…" observed Chad.

"Do you think it works the other way round?" I asked. "And every time you stuck that knife in him a little wooden effigy somewhere cried out in pain?"

We laughed. Plumstead didn't.

"Look, the dirty bastard pissed himself in the back."

"Why did we have to use my fucking motor?" grumbled Chad.

"I'll get the garage to give it a spring clean for you, on the firm," said Plumstead.

Chad nodded. "Thanks."

"Just as well we never came in Sonia's mini," Plumstead said. "I'd be on a sex ban for a month."

"You should have had his wallet off him for damages, Chad," I said.

"Here it is," he replied, throwing it over. "Back pocket job."

I caught it. "Quite a wad, Marky boy. And look, a couple of grams and some Es in here and all. Result!"

"Well save that for later," said Plumstead. "This is where we have to get serious. We're going to catch ourselves a giant ginger cunt without a net. Let's hope he's in the Northy. It's a lot less busy there than it is outside of the Tiger's Head."

"Mark," said Chad. "When did you open this bag of Revels?"

"Where did you find it?"

"Under the passenger seat."

"April."

"Great." Chad opened the bag even more and poured the remains into his mouth. Plumstead waited for him to eat them and added "April, 1988."

"You fucking piece of shit."

We laughed all the way down the Old Kent Road.

***

As we drove past the Lord Northbrook pub in Burnt Ash Road, I noticed Fatty Lol was standing outside, necking his traditional pint of lager top and chatting to a fit blonde bird who was busy lighting a fag.

"Pull up in Micheldever Road, Plum," I said, "First left."

When he had parked, I said. "Now, I'm not trying to take over but I know the geezer with the tart who was outside double well – it was Fatty Lol, Mr South London West Ham himself. Now I know that you both know him too, but Lol knows that you're connected to the Iron Army whereas he thinks I'm a one-man band. So, if I approach him…"

"You can ask him if Jacko is inside…"

"And no alarm bells will ring. He'll trust me – especially if I say I've got a trade that Roberts might be interested in."

"And because he trusts you, Jacko will trust you…"

"Exactly my thinking. Right, leave it to me."

***

Fatty Lol was almost over-pleased to see me and very obligingly brought Jacko out of the saloon bar. As I suspected, Roberts was extremely keen on examining the various parcels I said I had in my boot – snide whisky, Russian firearms and a kilo of Chas "straight off the brick". He bought my story when I said Ray Pearce had suggested that I put a bit of business his way, and he took no notice of the tall, thickset black man we passed on the way to Chad's car. He wasn't even aware of him when I opened the boot and Chad's cosh connected with his temple.

Roberts didn't wake up until we were through the tunnel.

"What I can't understand," said Chad slowly. "Is why Millwall mugs are drinking in a West Ham boozer."

"It's not a West Ham pub, it's where The Business drink," explained Plumstead. "You know, the punk band. 'Harry May' and all that."

"And their following are all football geezers who love the music," I added. "Even Schitzy gets in there."

"Chelsea Schitzy?"

"The very same."

"Fuck me."

"He probably would if he'd drunk enough and you stuck a blue and white syrup on," said Plumstead

"Did you clock that blonde with Lol outside the Northy?" I asked dreamily. "Sandra Bigg, the one with the fag on? I would lay on top of her until the neighbours called the council to complain about the smell."

"I don't know where you get the energy," said Plumstead with a grin. He glanced back at Chad and carried on, "I was hanging about outside his drum this morning because he was dropping some dopy bird off from last night, one of the dancers. She was blonde and all."

"The tall one?"

"Yeah."

"What was she like between the sheets, Aitch?"

"Wet, mate. Fanny like a fairground waterslide."

Plumstead laughed so much he almost hit the 97 bus to Chingford in front.

***

Jacko Roberts squinted as he came round. His head throbbed and there was a bright 150-watt light shining directly into his face. He couldn't see where he was or who was with him. All he knew was that he was sitting upright in a chair and that the floor was concrete – he could feel that because he had no shoes and socks on. A garage maybe? The back of his head ached like buggery and there was a slight pinching pain in his testicles that he couldn't reach down and scratch because his arms were tied tightly to the arms of the chair. Jesus wept.

Jacko groaned. He had some kind of plastic sheeting over his legs but the draft suggested that his trousers and underwear had also been removed.

As he fidgeted, the blinding light was moved away and Jacko blinked faces into focus.

"Good afternoon, Mr Roberts," said a man with long hair and a beaming smile. "Welcome to East London. I've been expecting you. My name is Terence Bishop – you may have heard of me. I think you know a friend of ours, Donald Warwick, popularly known as Mungo. I need you tell me what you know about his disappearance."

"I don't know nothing," spluttered Roberts. "I don't know the geezer, my life. I mean I've heard of him from football but we've never met."

A sharp pain erupted in his right testicle.

Terry Bishop shook his head. "You should know that I don't like liars, Jacko. Your part in Mungo's murder has already been turned into a little folksong by your compatriots at the Den. You've been grassed up by your mates. Now, you should also know that the nasty pain you've just experienced is level two on a dial that goes up to eleven. It should have been ten but we're rock stars and we love a bit of Spinal Tap, know what I mean?"

He paused. "Do you know the Richardsons, Jacko? Charles and Eddie? Of course you do. They're South London boys so you know *of* them at the very least. I've had the privilege of knowing Charlie personally since 1984, ever since he came out of the shovel. He's a bright man, smart and funny. He smokes too much but the mind..." – he tapped the side of his head – "the mind is as sharp as a cut-throat razor. Now, Charles and Eddie have always denied the charges that they tortured their victims by pumping an electric charge into their bollocks. But you know as well as I do that they did do it. Of course they fuckin' did. They also used whips on them, lobbed off their toes with bolt cutters and stubbed their fags out on their arms."

Jacko squirmed in his chair. There were four other men there, including the mug who'd lured him out of the Northy. Harry

Tyler, Lol had called him. So, a Harry, a Terry, he'd listen for other names. There was nothing he liked better than revenge.

Jacko realised Terry was watching him as he was trying to take in all the details of the garage that they were in. He took another zap to the gonads and cried out in pain.

"It's no use screaming, son," the gangster said amiably. "Nobody will hear you and it'll piss me off. Capisce? Or should that be *capire*? How's your Italian, Jack? Better than your memory, I hope."

Terry spoke slowly, to build the fear. He was enjoying every moment of this, I could tell.

"Charlie's victims used to bleed so much that their clothes were ruined by their own blood. He would have to lend them his own clobber so they could get home afterwards. People called it 'taking a shirt from Charlie'. I've got a spare dicky here that should fit you perfectly, and an old pair of strides too. So if you're a good boy, Jacko, you won't be going home stark bollock naked. See, I'm a nice guy, basically, but I am a bit twisted. The idea of a spot of casual torture has always appealed to me, and I'd quite happily do all of that to you – stubbing fags out on your face, clipping yer Bromleys, electrifying your plums and so on. I would happily do that all day long until you were begging to grass up everyone you ever knew, loved or cared about… if I had the time. But you see Jacko, time you see is very much of the essence today. A lot of scores need to be settled quickly. So I'm fully prepared to accelerate the process."

He nodded at Plumstead who gave him another electric shock. Jacko screamed.

"That was a four, and as I said it goes all the way up to eleven with that funny old Spinal Tap twist. So it will hurt like buggery and probably ruin your chances of ever having kids. Some would say that would be doing society a favour by stopping you from procreating… a few less mindless Millwall motherfuckers on the manor."

He paused. A car pulled up outside. Terry smiled.

"But even with the electric shock therapy might take too long with a thick mug like you, Roberts. So I've decided to bring in an old friend of the family to speed things up. He was a friend of Charlie and Eddie's too. The Richardsons used to call him their A-bomb."

The garage doors opened. Outside, One-Gin stood back and let his passenger walk in first. He was an older man, wearing a three-piece Italian suit, a classic shirt and a silk tie. He had his overcoat draped over his shoulders.

"This immaculately dressed gentleman is known as The Dentist," Terry continued. "He is Mr Fraser. You might know him better as Mad Frankie but you'd be wise not to call him that to his face. As you can see, Mr Fraser has brought his tools. Thank you, Frankie."

"My pleasure, Terence."

Frankie Fraser removed his overcoat and jacket and gave them to One-Gin. Then he removed his cufflinks and rolled up his sleeves, slowly, very slowly. Finally he opened his metal attaché case.

It was another piece of theatre designed to scare the shit out of Roberts. I watched the scene play out knowing full well there was nothing I could do to make it end well.

Fraser nodded that he was ready, and gave Chad a dental gag to clamp open Jacko's mouth. The big man stood back. Mad Frankie produced a stainless-steel scaler.

"Just my little starter," he said, without a smile.

It took Frankie Fraser no longer than ninety seconds to get Jacko to talk, and by then the 'patient' was literally spitting blood onto the plastic sheeting that covered his legs.

"Please," he begged. "No more. Please."

"Wise decision," said Terry. "Now tell me, this little murder spree of yours, was this just a football thing or was there another motive? Think carefully and answer truthfully because I can smell lies."

"It, it, was a job," Jacko stuttered. "I was hired to do it. P-p-paid, I was paid."

"Who by?"

Roberts hesitated. Frankie Fraser loomed over him with a sickle probe.

Jacko recoiled. "A couple of geezers out of Surrey. Camberley. They contacted us via a little firm down the Old Kent Road. We were contracted."

"What did they pay you, out of interest?"

"A grand."

Bishop's face clouded up. "All this fucking aggro for a poxy bag of sand? Hit the buzzer, Chad."

Jacko screamed. Terry composed himself.

"Sorry, I lost it there. But killing my top boys for one large just adds insult to injury. Don't worry, we won't zap you again as long as you keep talking. Now, tell me everything you know about this pair of clowns from Camberley."

"Uh, they were bikers, Gypsy Jokers, they said. No, Gypsy Rebels. They came on proper hogs, Harleys, to the Sydney Arms in Chislehurst for the meet. Scruffy cunts in leathers with greasy barnets. In their forties. They said they were ex-paras."

"Did they say what the hit was about?"

"Gear, yeah, they said gear, but we were to make it look like it was a football thing."

"And did they say who they were working for?"

"Yeah, a guy called Davies, Benny Davies."

"That's their leader, real name Kevin," said One-Gin. "Falklands veteran. Hard as nails. He's got a garage on the outskirts of Farnborough."

"Have they paid you yet?"

"Yeah, a monkey up front, and a monkey after. I met 'em in the Sid again last night."

"Well thank you, Jacko. You've been most helpful. You can get dressed now. Wungy, get him that spare clobber out of the front room please, and give him some gel to stop the gums bleeding."

Roberts added the names Wungy and Chad to his revenge list.

"So you're done with me? I can go?" There was a note of disbelief in his voice.

"Just one more thing. What were the odds when you took out Mungo and Jimmy?"

"Ten to two. Well, ten to one really because the first one, Jimmy, he was coshed before it even started."

"And how many did Mungo do for?"

"He knocked five of us clean out before we got him. One of the boys is still in intensive care. I've never seen anything like it. He was like a lion."

Terry smiled. That pleased him. "Thank you, Jacko. You've been very honest and you've told me what I wanted to know. Untie him Aitch, and give eye to him for a minute."

Aitch, thought Jacko. That's Harry Tyler again. He also had Wungy's name, the weasel-faced one; Terry Bishop of course. And the big black geezer was Chad. He would not forget. He would rip these cow-sons to shreds.

I breathed a side of relief inwardly. At least I wouldn't be party to a cold-blooded murder today. I released Jacko's restraints and when One-Gin came back with the clothes I removed the plastic sheeting from his lap and helped him to his feet. His bollocks were as black as Newgate's knocker. He was shaking while he got dressed.

"Now Jacko," said Terry. "We're going to have a put a hood over your head so you can't spot any clues to our location. And we'll put you in cuffs for the journey home, for the safety of our driver."

Roberts nodded. He seemed grateful.

"Here, take these for your pain."

Terry Bishop scooped a glass of water and two pills from a near-by work top. Jacko gulped them down greedily. Terry turned to Chad. "Drop him off back in South London, will you Chad?"

The big man grunted.

"Okay," said Terry. "One-Gin will drop Mr Fraser back to Islington and give him a nice drink for his trouble – thank you Frank." He shook Mad Frankie's hand and turned back to us.

"Now Plumstead, you need to set off down to Bristol. You won't have Chad for back-up now, so do you want to take Harry?"

"Will you be okay, Tel?" I asked. "That leaves you on your Jack."

"Yeah, it's fine, it's only for a couple of hours. Nobody knows about this place and it's more heavily fortified than Hitler's bunker."

"We were in Chad's car," said Plumstead. "Is there another motor we can take?"

"Take the Alfa Romeo SZ over the road. It's the red one. The keys are under the wheel, front left. Oh, but Mark, a quick word."

Terry pulled Plumstead into a corner and spoke to him softly but quickly. Mark nodded and left to open up the car boot while Bishop walked into the house.

Plumstead then climbed into the driving seat. Me and Spider got in too, Spider up front, me in the back. Terry reappeared carrying a cardboard box. He put it in the boot, closed it and gave Plumstead a thumbs up.

"What was that about?" I asked.

"Oh, it's just another little job we've got to do on the way back tonight. It won't take long."

I nodded. "Cool."

We set off for the M25 with AC/DC's 'Dirty Deeds Done Dirt Cheap' playing on the car stereo, "I was quite surprised that Terry let Jacko live," I said after a while. "I thought he was brown bread there for sure."

"Oh yeah," said Plumstead. "He'll be on Terry's Christmas card list now and get backstage passes to all the shows."

He and Spider laughed out loud.

"Of course, he ain't letting him live, you plum," Plumstead said finally. "It's just Tel playing his little psychological games. Roberts won't last the night mate, and whatever happens to him the world will have to know about it because Terry needs to send out that message."

I felt such a twat.

**

The death of John "Jacko" Roberts made front page news on Tuesday, thirty-six and a half hours later. The "pain-killers" had actually been strong sleeping tablets. When Roberts came round in the early hours of Monday morning, he was flat on his back on a building site close to Millwall's Den. He was naked, his hands had been nailed to the floor, and his body had been scarred with a series of small cuts. He died slowly, and in great pain, at around 5am that same morning. His body was discovered by a Polish building worker two and a half hours later. The initials IKL – for Irons Kill Lions – had been carved into his forehead.

Chapter Nine

Sunday, May 27, 1990.

We pulled in at Reading service station for a takeaway burger and chips. I made the excuse that I had to ring Jenny to cancel tonight's shenanigans and called Mark Nixson instead.

"Just a quick update, guv, I can't stop. First off, they got hold of Jacko Roberts, the bloke who murdered Mungo, so you're likely to have another corpse wash up soon. Things have changed. I'm not with Terry Bishop tonight. Three of us are on our way to Bristol on a mission that doesn't seem to involve explosives."

"So do I need to put a surveillance team on Bishop?"

"I don't think so. He's at the Walthamstow safehouse, in Norfolk Road, and I don't think he'll be moving until tomorrow when we have to do the ransom exchange to pick up Wolf, that's in Chislehurst. Have you got a pen?"

"Yeah,"

"It's a place called the Old Forge in Manor Park. It's at the end of a cul-de-sac, one way in, one way out."

"So we could set up a surveillance camera?" Nixson mused.

"My thought exactly. And maybe plot up an armed response unit close by, just in case it gets messy."

"Yes. What time, Harry?"

"Sorry, 10am on the dot. Terry is to go alone on his bike, so he'll stand out. We'll be there around the corner."

"How many?"

"Guv, can't stop…"

Plumstead and Spider were a few feet away loaded up with burgers, fries and Cokes.

"Oi, oi, if he says he's loves you, he's fucking lying," guffawed Plumstead.

"She says you're a pig," I replied, hanging up the phone.

***

Four hours later we were plotted up in a posh street in Clifton, about forty yards from one of the houses Plumstead had previously staked out. We'd been there for some time.

"What's Spider waiting for?" I groaned.

"The downstairs light to be turned off. That's the signal apparently."

"Nice drum."

"It's about the size of Tel's over in Chigwell. You've got to see it, Aitch, he's fucking caked now."

"Strewth. A bit different from where he started then. Over Mile End way, wasn't it?"

"More Bow. You know him and Wolfy had to share a bed when they were kids?"

"I didn't."

"Then when Wolf started school he used to get anxious and piss the bed at night."

"Really?"

"Ask Terry. He said he pissed it so much there was a rainbow down the end of it."

I laughed loudly at that. "That's when old man Bishop went and bought 'em bunk beds. He's tucked up in Tower Hamlet cemetery now…"

"Big Terry?"

"Yeah, it's their mother Ethel you want to worry about."

"The old dear I met at the Athena?"

"Yeah."

"Why do they call her The Profit?"

"It's Prophet with a p-h. Don't you know that story?"

I shook my head and laughed. "That's One-Gin's accent for you."

"It was Mrs Bishop who sniffed out that fuckin' no-good Filth infiltrator we had last month. Terry must have told you? She met him once, shook his hand, stared at him, and just said 'You're a wrong'un, bad auras. You're filth.' She just blurted it straight out. Well of course the geezer denied it but it proper freaked him out, you could tell. So Terry had him checked out with our friends on the force, bent Old Bill, and bingo. Goodnight Vienna."

I took all that in, showing no emotion, and steered the conversation back to death. "You ever think about where you want to be buried, Mark?"

"I'm not having the worms take me, mate, I'm gonna be burnt and have me ashes scattered in Sainsbury's carpark."

I gave him a quizzical look. "Why?"

"Cos I've spent so long in me car waiting for Sonia, her indoors, to do the shopping there, I've come to consider the place a home from fucking home. Seriously, Son could turn buying a loaf and six eggs into a half an hour mission…"

We both chuckled. "What was Terry's wife like? The first one?"

"Thelma? Lovely woman. Bethnal Green girl, hard as nails, you wouldn't want a right-hander off her."

"What happened there then?"

"Sylvie came along a couple of years ago. She was stunning, she was useful, and she must be fucking good in bed coze within a couple of months Thelma got the old Spanish archer. He just traded her in for a new model. Thelma's family never forgave him, but what were they going to do? A guy like that. There's nothing they could do."

"You know what I could do with – a coffee."

"Me too, mate. We'll stop somewhere on the way back."

I looked around us. The streets were completely deserted in every direction.

"You been to his Chigwell place?"

"It's the dog's, Aitch. And, he's just had a swimming pool installed in the back garden in the shape of a coffin."

"You're taking the piss."

"My life, it's 30ft long and about 20ft at its widest. Heated and all."

Suddenly, in the distance a cacophony of police sirens ruptured the silence.

"Shit," I said.

"That will be the distraction," Plumstead replied.

"Distraction?"

"Smoke and mirrors, mate. While the crusties are kicking off in town, we'll be in and out with the plunder."

"You sound like a fucking pirate."

"Look, Spider's over the wall. Game on."

***

Spider dropped to his haunches and stayed still. The grounds of the house were huge but he had deliberately climbed into the part that was the most heavily wooded. He took out his binoculars and studied the house carefully. Not a soul was moving. The upstairs lights had just been turned off too, which meant that the old cunt was curled up in bed. He knew he was alone.

Spider decided to stay still a few minutes – just as a precaution. He would have waited longer but the place gave him the creeps. He was a city boy born and bred and hated every inch of the countryside. He didn't like the sound of the wind in the trees, and the strange shrieks and calls of unknown nocturnal wildlife. And he especially didn't like the loud, eerie *"Yaaggaghh"* sound of foxes in the distance. They sounded almost human. No, not human; more ghostly.

Spider gave it five minutes. No movement. That was enough. He was just about to move forward when he heard a twig snap behind him.

Someone was there. Filth? Thinking fast he turned to corner the intruder. He was small. A kid? It was too dark to see much more than a flash of black and white. Spider felt a sharp pain in his hand and cried out. But there was no one there now. Whoever it was had gone. He staggered out onto the lawn and wrapped his handkerchief around the wound. What the fuck?

Shit. Spider stayed stock still. If the old bastard had heard him, it would be game over. But no lights came on. He put on his night vision googles and made his way down to the French windows about 100 feet ahead of him. They were unlocked as promised. Slowly and carefully, Spider edged his way out of the front room and turned to his right. The door at the end of the

151

hall was supposed to be the study, and luckily it was. It too was unlocked. Inside, a large Monet copy was hanging proudly on the wall. Behind that was the safe. He took the snide Monet down and clicked in the combination – the idiot owner's birthday! He heard the lock undo. He pulled it open and felt inside. Yep, there it was – the real Monet, neatly rolled. two million quid's worth of oil painting right there in his mitt...

Spider momentarily considered not going back to the car, but the risks of going against the Bishops were too great. He left the house as quickly and quietly as he could and pelted over to the exterior wall – he wouldn't risk the clump of trees again. He just rested the painting on the top, hauled himself over and jogged back to the car. Nobody saw him because nobody was there.

"All go to plan?" asked Plumstead as Spider climbed into the back seat and sighed with relief.

"Yeah, except I got stabbed by some little cunt."

"Stabbed?"

"Yeah."

"In the house?"

"No, in the fuckin' wooded bit, in some bushes."

"What did he look like?"

"I couldn't see him, I didn't have the bins on. I just caught a flash of black and white and then I felt a proper stab of pain. Look!"

He removed the handkerchief and showed us the gash on his hand.

"How tall was he?"

"Not big. Fucking fast though. He was on his knees. I thought I'd cornered him but he moved like lightning."

"Hold on," I said. "A little black and white bastard that lashed out when you cornered it? That's not a person you twat, that was a fuckin' badger."

I turned on the internal light. "Look at the cut, Spide. It's a claw mark not a knife cut!"

Plumstead roared. "Black and white, you melt! You made it sound like you'd been mugged by the fucking Specials."

"Well," I sang, "This town is coming like a Ghost Town."

"Listen, it was dark, and it was quick, and it fucking hurt," said Spider sulkily.

"Fucking Muppet."

"You were probably near its sett," I said.

"At least Harry only gets ravaged by friendly beavers..." laughed Plumstead. "Big, wet, hairy ones."

"That's funny. Yeah, pick on Tyler for a change. It's all right for you two mugs sitting in the car. I'm the one taking all the risks."

Plumstead gave a look of fake concern. "Are you okay for the next two jobs, Spider, or do we need to call in Johnny Morris and Terry fuckin' Nutkins as back-up?"

"I'm fine," he said, still grumpy. "I just need to stop the blood."

"Here," said Plumstead slinging him serviettes from the burger bag. "Use these. Muppet."

***

The first bomb had exploded at 9.30pm at a Barclays Bank in the city centre. No one was hurt but extensive damage was done. Two other bombs, at Bristol County Bank and Coutts were equally effective.

Bristol police scrambled to investigate the attacks but were hampered by a large mob of animal rights protestors who were staging an unauthorised demonstration through the high street, shutting off Bristol Bridge and Baldwin Street to traffic. At the same time, angry youth in the near-by St Paul's district began looting shops and over-turning cars. The 'distraction' was in full swing.

Victoria Boosler was nowhere near the action. She was outside the Benston Institute with Tim Robb whose grand plan was to blow the research laboratory to kingdom come. Tim had already used Semtex to take out the near-by electrical substation, so the Institute sat in darkness.

She approached the gate on foot. Old Reg wasn't on duty but another near look-alike – Reg 3 – was, a similar gormless lump of lard, muscle and bloody-mindedness in an ill-fitting uniform. He spotted her and opened the window of the security lodge.

"What do you want?" he barked, as friendly as a rattlesnake.

"I'm so sorry," she said, in her best little-girl-lost voice. "It's my Peugeot, it's conked out down the road. It's probably nothing but don't know anything about engines and I really couldn't face a night out here in the darkness. Can you take a look at it for me? I would be so grateful."

He pulled a face.

"I can pay you. Look, I have £100 here in cash. If you help me it's yours."

The guard's eyes lit up. "Hold on," he said, shutting the window. He left the lodge and walked out towards her. "You're lucky it's so quiet tonight. I can spare you a few min…"

Crack. Tim Robb emerged from the shadows and knocked him unconscious with a truncheon. The pair walked through the security gate, bypassing the large electric ones, and headed towards the Institute.

Victoria knew that Robb was wearing a rucksack containing the remainder of the Semtex. She also knew that a team of armed spooks were in place ready to make sure he none of it was detonated.

What she didn't know was that the building was not as deserted as it appeared. Harvey Mendelssohn, to escape his wife for the day, had just finished twelve hours of painstaking lab work when the lights went out. He had then slowly made his way out of the building. He emerged just as Robb and Victoria approached in their night goggles.

"Oh, here's a bonus," snarled Tim, pulling out the Luger Victoria didn't know he had.

"Mendelssohn!" he yelled. "Animal killer! Drop to your fuckin' knees."

"Tim, don't do anything stupid," said Victoria.

"Stupid? No. This is what I was born to do."

Mendelssohn reluctantly complied with the order. Robb walked towards him.

"I always thought the best way for me to dispose of you would be to get you in an abattoir and subject you to the same kind of torture that you inflict on defenceless animals," he smiled. "But sometimes fate plays things differently. Here you are, and here am I, and here's my gun…"

"I'm not scared of thugs like you," said Mendelssohn.

"Well, you should be," replied Tim, raising the gun and aiming at his forehead.

"Tim, don't," said Victoria. She moved towards him. Robb pointed the gun at her.

"Stay back, Vicky!" he snapped. "Stay well clear!"

He turned back towards Harvey Mendelssohn and lifted the gun again.

"This is for…"

The four gunshots that followed were all on target. Mendelssohn had soiled his trousers but he was unharmed. Tim Robb in contrast was on the floor leaking like a colander. Victoria felt nothing, except relief.

***

We pulled up at the next fancy mansion and I couldn't help myself.

"Take care Spider mate," I said, waiting a beat before I added, "This one's got ferrets."

Plumstead laughed. "Two of them up yer strides mate and you'll be praying for Brock the Badger."

"Ha, fuckin' ha."

This job was quicker. He was over the fence and in and out through a downstairs window, emerging with a pricey pair of late 19th century Italian rococo figures in a hold-all. They were Venetian blackamoor statues, apparently, hand carved in sycamore wood, and standing on rococo gilt plinths. Current value? Just shy of £10K.

"Lovely job," said Plumstead. "The last target is just around the corner."

"This will be the easiest," said Spider. "Back door unlocked, first door on the right, a fuckin' Warhol hanging on the wall. Leave the car running."

Spider moved quickly but was a lot faster coming back with a pair of Dobermans barking their heads off and a home owner firing buckshot at his arse from an upstairs window.

"When did he get the fuckin' dogs?" gasped Spider as Plumstead drove off at high speed. "Nobody mentioned dogs!"

"Did you get the Warhol?"

Spider proudly held up the framed Endangered Species screen print.

"Fuck me, a panda!" I exclaimed. "You're lucky that didn't bite."

"Weren't there supposed to be two of them?" asked Plumstead.

"Fuck off."

"Seriously, Tel wanted two."

"Are you joking? I ain't fucking going back."

"No, he said there were two because the buyer wanted them to fucking mate."

"Fuck off."

At the scene of the crime an irate homeowner was screaming down the phone at the police operator who told him politely but firmly that she was sorry but no officers were currently available to investigate the theft of his precious Warhol print.

When we reached the M4, Plumstead turned on the news to hear shocking reports of the mindless chaos that had brought

Bristol to a standstill. There was also breaking news of a fatal shooting at nearby Clifton.

"What happens to all this gear now?" I asked.

"I'll drive it on to the slaughter in Walthamstow, and Tel will keep it in the safe until the inquiry fizzles out. There's a buyer waiting in the Dam for the lot so we'll just take it over to him on the little European tour we do as a warm-up for the Yank dates."

"Cool."

"If there's a tour. We ain't got Wolfie back yet," muttered Spider.

"How hard do you think it is to get another singer?" Plumstead said with a laugh. "I mean, Paul Di'Anno's not doing much is he? If the worst happens to Wolf, do you really think Tel will break up the band? The band is bigger than any individual band member. Five will get you ten he's already got Henry sussing out replacements."

With that, he slid a Guns N' Roses album into the cassette player and put his foot down. An hour and ten minutes later we screeched to a halt outside a garage on the outskirts of Farnborough called Gypsy Repairs.

Plumstead got out of the car and walked over to the building, checking it for signs of life. When he was satisfied no one was about, he removed Terry Bishop's box from the boot and then came to show us the bottle that had rested securely inside.

"A Molly," he said. "A Molotov cocktail. You light this bit of cloth, attached here to the stopper, chuck it at the target and BOOM. I've been waiting all me life to throw one of these babies."

"How does it work?" asked Chad.

"The wick is soaked in kerosene, the liquid inside is petrol. When it hits the target the bottle smashes and every drop of it goes up in flames. Watch."

He got out of the car, walked to about ten feet away from the garage front, lit the cloth wick with his lighter and hurled it at the target.

By the time he was back in the driving seat the garage belonging to the Gypsy Rebels was a raging inferno.

***

At 12.45am Plumstead dropped me back to Narrow Street. Jobs done. I didn't feel like sleeping so I walked over to my motors and got the Sunday papers out of the back. Up in the flat I made myself a cheese roll, opened a can of Fosters and sat down for a read.

A picture from Mark Brennan's funeral had made the front page of the Sunday Telegraph. The caption threw to a think-piece inside about the need to restore capital punishment for the murder of police officers.

The rest of the photos showed a strong turn-out of uniformed plod, with hundreds of wreaths on display. But it was Brennan's widow Sandra who caught my eye. She was tall, dignified, and beautiful – an absolute stunner. Her dark hair was cropped short, and she had knock-out cheekbones. She wasn't smiling but you could see the good Mrs Brennan had laughed a lot in her life. Those cheekbones were something else – high and quite magnificent. They reminded me a lot of Joni Mitchell. I looked at her twice to make sure I didn't know her. Then I realised I did. For two reasons. Firstly, because I'm pretty sure that when I had to give a talk to some would-be u/c operatives a couple of years ago there was a woman with those same incredible features down the front. Her barnet was different then, but the zygomatic bones were identical.

Secondly, put a long blonde wig on the widow and she was the dead spit of Wolf Bishop's new girlfriend, Vanessa – the woman who had allegedly been kidnapped at the same time as he had.

Mark Brennan's wife had been ex-Old Bill, Roy Pryor had told me that when we first spoke about this job in Didcot. Could Nessa be Sandra Brennan working undercover, not for us but for herself, for revenge? When justice fails you, what have you got left other than resignation... or vengeance?

I set the alarm for 7am and hit the sack but didn't sleep much.

Chapter Ten

Monday, May 28, 1990.

At 7am, I made a coffee and called Mark Nixson's funny old brick phone.

"Guv, there's been a complication," I said. "I don't think that the person who kidnapped Wolf is anything to do with Millwall football hooligans or disgruntled biker gangsters. I think it's Mark's widow. Check out the pictures, her features are identical. And she's ex-Old Bill isn't she? Ex-UC, Roy Pryor said. I don't think she wants money — she's put the ransom demand out there just to flush Terry out. What I think she wants is just revenge, plain and simple."

"Christ," said Mark Nixson. I could almost hear the cogs of brains working as he thought this twist out. "I can picture the resemblance from the surveillance shots of her with Wolf... Shit on a shitty stick. I never saw that coming. Thanks Harry. We will check that out right now and re-think our tactics. We will still have our snipers in place in a house opposite the Old Forge — the owners were very co-operative. In fact the armed response team should be in there now, getting set up. I'll warn them of the possibility that the kidnapper is Mark Brennan's widow. There will also be a SWAT team on stand-by."

I bought the morning papers on the way to Stratford and flicked through them quickly. The news pages were eaten up with the Bristol riots – and the death of Tim Robb had inspired a demonstration against "state brutality" that was due to take place there this afternoon, the usual ragbag of anarchists, wannabe Maoists, animal rights groups and CND activists bolstered by students from the University of Bristol and Bristol Poly. There was nothing on the robberies but there was a small, apparently unrelated news story about the brutal murder of known East End felon Don Warwick.

Presumably the arson attack in Farnborough would make the London *Evening Standard*.

Elsewhere *The Sun* had a spread on the kidnapping of Wolf Bishop complete with the Bizarre column editor's reverential tribute to Wolf Bishop: "one of the most distinctive voices in modern British rock" and "the UK's answer to Axl Rose".

***

I got to the Athena Apollo at 9am. Terry was up in the office with One-Gin. In front of him were two differently coloured lines of powder and a steaming cup of black coffee.

"What you on, Tel?"

"Old Wungy's wake-up breakfast special – cocaine, caffeine and amphetamine."

"So if you can't out-shoot the Grim Reaper today at least you can outrun him."

Terry laughed loudly. "Where are the others? It's time to go."

"Sounds like they're downstairs," said One-Gin.

They were – Plumstead, Spider, Chad, the ever-scowling Psycho Manny and some new kid called Tesco Eddie. We were eight-handed. Terry nodded and demolished his breakfast. One-Gin opened the mobile arsenal and I helped myself to an Israeli Desert Eagle with a 14-inch barrel. Like a Magnum but more powerful. It was the best weapon there.

We went down to the bar area and he laid out a map of Chislehurst on a table.

"Now this," he said, "is how it's going to be…"

***

At 9.58am, a lone biker in a black, battered Bell Bullitt motorbike helmet and matching black leather jacket drove his Norton Commando cautiously to the end of Manor Park and parked outside the Old Forge.

The rest of us were plotted up a couple of hundred yards to his rear, safely out of sight. The biker sat patiently until 10am when a loud distorted voice boomed from an upstairs window: "Put the money inside the gate."

"I want to see the hostages," the biker hollered back. "I need to see that they're safe."

The door of the Old Forge opened and out stumbled Wolf Bishop and Vanessa. They had gags over their mouths and their hands strapped behind their backs, but they were recognisably the hostages.

The lone biker dismounted and walked quickly to the sturdy wooden gate which he opened. Then he deposited a bulky hold-all by the hedge in the front garden.

"It's all there," he said.

"It had better be". Vanessa's gag was no longer in her mouth and her hands were no longer behind her back. She was holding a Browning Buck Mark in her right hand and pointing it directly at the biker. The man turned and ran. "Not fast enough, Terry," muttered Sandra Brennan. She fired twice and he hit the deck, and then she turned and shot Wolf Bishop three times at point-blank range.

At that precise moment two things happened. A car containing Terry Bishop roared to a stop outside the Old Forge and a police loud hailer announced, "ARMED POLICE! Drop your weapons!"

Terry was out of the car and moving fast. He shot Vanessa/Sandra straight in the chest and then turned and opened fire at the upper windows of the house opposite. Police marksmen Colin Edmonds and Alan Wightman turned out to be the better shots.

In less than a minute, Wolf and Terry Bishop and their kidnapper Sandra Brennan were all down and out; as dead as dogs in a ditch.

The masked biker on the floor however appeared to be twitching.

"GET OUT OF THE CAR WITH YOUR HANDS IN THE AIR," commanded the man with the loud hailer. We did as we were told, me, Plumstead, Chad, Tesco Eddie and Spider looking like kids playing a POW game.

Armed cops came and took away our guns.

An unmarked estate car pulled up containing DI Mark Nixson. He surveyed the carnage, smiled, and said "What a great start to my week."

He turned to the armed unit and said "Get these five plums to Bromley nick and make sure they are kept well apart. I'll be along to take their statements personally."

The biker groaned. Nixson pulled off his helmet to reveal One-Gin. "Ah, Mr Denny...disguised as Terry Bishop to confuse the kidnapper... known to you as Nessa; real name Sandra Brennan, the widow of one of your last victims."

One-Gin scowled. Mark Nixson took a deep breath and held it in his lungs as if smelling the perfect justice of the scenes. "I of course believe in the letter of the law, but there are some among us who would say revenge is sweet... sweeter when it's delivered by an avenging angel. The mighty macho Bishops brought down by a weak, feeble woman... with the heart and stomach of a king. I'll be laughing at that thought for years."

As we were driven off, uniform and scene of crime officers began to arrive. Nixson allowed himself one last smile and then headed back to his vehicle for the four-mile drive to Bromley.

***

We were separated at the station. I was taken directly to Nixson.

"A result," he said shaking my hand.

"A partial one. A shame about Sandra and a shame the two bastards won't stand trial."

"But on the plus side the Bishops are out of action."

"Not yet. What's left of the gang still have assets guv, and you need to hit the Walthamstow slaughter fast before the art from last night leaves the country."

He nodded. "So all of that anarchy in Bristol was just a cover for a major heist?"

"I think so. Although I still can't figure out what connected Robb to the Bishops. I wonder if Victoria got anything on that."

"Boosler?"

"Yeah."

"She was with Robb when he got shot last night."

"You mean Tim Robb is…"

"Brown bread as you Cock-en-ee lot say."

"How did it happen?"

"He was shot while he was attempting to execute the chief scientist at the Benston Institute. The spooks took him out."

"And Victoria?"

"She's as good as gold, I'm told."

"Thank God."

"You didn't realise Vanessa was Sandra Brennan."

"Nope. I recognised her – it was the cheekbones more than anything. But couldn't place her. She clocked me though."

"Listen Harry, what do you say that all four of us get together off the manor at the weekend – you, me, Roy and Shirley Kelly – to drink to our success, or should I say your success? Yours and Victoria's? Maybe we should invite her too."

"I'm game."

"We'll do the debrief after we've interviewed those four toe-rags. We're just waiting for their brief."

"Henry?"

"Yeah. Okay. How did Wungy survive getting shot at close range?"

"Body armour. But he knocked himself out when he fell."

"Of course. So if your boys hadn't been over the road, Bishop would have shot Sandra dead and got away with it."

"Yes, again thanks to you. What will you do later today?"

"Get back to Wapping and pack. I've got one more night there and then I'd better use up some holiday time. I hear Porta Banus is nice this time of year."

***

I was still high when I got back to Wapping and didn't fancy spending my last night in the East End alone. The question was who to invite as company? I'd met some incredible women in the last few weeks. Tough but beautiful Tasmin, soft but loveable Jenny, the unknown quantity that was Sid's flirty girlfriend Ena… Victoria would probably drive up if I invited her… Then I made up my mind.

At 8pm, I was sitting by the back window of Booty's Riverside Bar in Narrow Street, sipping a Whisky Sour and watching the waves when I heard a woman's voice behind me.

"Why Mr Tyler," she said. "Fancy seeing you here."

I looked up. She had a smile so wide it seemed to be hooked over her ears.

"Thanks for inviting me."

"Great to see you Shirley, what are you having?"

She looked me up and down and gave me a smaller, slyer smile.

"Why Harry," she said. "You, I hope."

POSTSCRIPT.

After Tim Robb's obituary in *The Daily Telegraph* revealed that he had been adopted, DI Mark Nixson asked me if I'd postpone my holiday and resume the identity of wayward activist Pete Harrison for long enough to attend his funeral "just in case" anything of note came to my attention.

I was hoping Victoria Boosler would be here, but no such luck. I didn't see any of Robb's anarchist army. Presumably the majority of the activists I had met had been arrested during the riots and were being held without bail pending their trials; so most of the mourners at the Holy Cross Catholic Church and at the South Bristol crem service were scruffy students rather than hardcore liberationists.

The exception was a scattering of well-dressed men at the front of the chapel. One elderly and obviously well-to-do gentleman sat stony-faced with his weeping wife. The other besuited men sat together but a few feet away from the first couple.

I recognised one of them instantly as Steven Knight – known and revered in London crime circles as "the Guv'nor" and assumed by the Metropolitan Police to be untouchable. Word was that if he were any further removed from the criminal coal face, he'd be the Archbishop of Canterbury.

Knight had been hands-on in the sixties, a proper Mod face leading his hard mob of young criminals out of the slums of Shoreditch to the rich pickings of the West End. That's when he went legit. He must be coming up for fifty now.

I had a quick look at the others when we filed out to see the wreaths. I presumed that the one who looked like him had to be his elder brother Kenny. The one who looked like Penfold was Henry Gibson. The other two? Muscle, probably.

But why were they here?

The newspaper photographers out to grab shots of weeping hippies didn't look twice at them. That's how successful the Knights had been in distancing themselves from notoriety. They were club owners, businessmen, property developers... utterly respectable. On the surface at least. But Steven Knight was also Terry Bishop's godfather. Was that another clue to a bigger picture?

Why would the Knights have come all the way from Chigwell in Essex to the funeral of an obscure soap dodger in Bristol? Try as I might, I could not see the connection. Robb had made his money from dealing. As far as I was aware the Knights were not now involved in the drugs trade, even at a distance.

After the service, I found a phone box and reported back.

"That's odd," said Mark Nixson. "Very odd."

"Guv, will you do me a favour and check out Tim Robb's background? If possible find out who adopted him and who his birth parents were? I don't know anything but that's the only thing I can think of that might just explain it."

I said I'd ring him back from the Costa. In the event he rang me the next day at the Marbella Club Hotel, once the private residence of Prince Alfonso of Hohenlohe-Langenburg don't you know?

Tim Robb's backstory turned out to be an extraordinary one. He was adopted by Bristol businessman Reginald Robb and his wife Suzanne – the old couple at the funeral – and educated at Clifton College, a local private school. His birth name was Sellers, his mother was Anthea Sellers, a one-time Swinging Sixties Mod model who had died of an overdose. Tim was her second son. The birth certificate did not name a father. But according to Rob McGibbon, a retired DCI who had specialised in the London crime gangs of the 1960s, the father of both of Anthea's sons was one Steven Knight.

Nixson explained, "I don't know, but I'm presuming that Knight tracked the boy down when he was in his teens and drew him into his circle. That's why he was pushing gear for

Terry Bishop – Knight's godson. They were all one big dysfunctional family."

"And his hatred of the Benston Institute?"

"That's the last piece of the puzzle and you'll kick yourself for not thinking of it. The MD of Benston Institute is one Reginald Robb."

"Tim's adoptive father?"

"The very same. The man who had given him everything all of his life, including a very expensive education. Now, it's possible that Robb really did hate animal cruelty with a vengeance but odds are the deeper motivation for the carnage he inflicted on the world was a simple pathological hatred of his father."

"I don't think he gave a flying fuck about the animal rights/veggie agenda. I reckon he adopted that philosophy purely because it helped cement his reputation with the crusty crowd who bought his dope and acid."

"You're a cynical man, Harry."

"A realist, guv. How many vegans do you see chomping on a Big Mac?"

"Still, case closed now."

"Except who were the people we robbed?"

"Reginald Robb, and two of his equally wealthy chums – good friends of the family, which is presumably how Tim Robb knew where the goodies were."

I nodded. That made sense. "There's just one other thing," I said.

"What's that?"

"Steven Knight is still at liberty."

"Well, that's one mountain that is not going to come to Mohammad, Harry."

"We'll see guv, we'll see."

POSTSCRIPT TWO:

The violent destruction of the Gypsy Repairs garage in Camberley lead to a police raid on the home of Gypsy Rebel gang leader Kevin "Benny" Davies. Among the weapons discovered were a quantity of Semtex, a pump-action shotgun normally used by US SWAT teams and several pipe bombs. He went on to face nine firearms and explosives charges with intent to endanger life. He was sentenced to life imprisonment.

*After the death of the Bishop brothers, Iron Hammer's manager and lawyer Henry Gibson announced that a live double album recorded at the band's final Stratford Town Hall concert would be rush-released in their memory, along with a video shot on the night containing backstage footage. The sympathetic rock press were quick to run the story that Terry Bishop had died heroically in a gunfight as he tried to rescue his kidnapped brother. Gibson maintained that the drug and theft allegations levelled at the band by the police and Fleet Street papers were actually the work of a rogue element within the band's roadcrew of which the Bishops had no knowledge. Furthermore, he announced that after their funerals, the band would start auditioning with a new singer and lead guitarist to "preserve and build on the band's incredible musical legacy...our US tour will go ahead; it's what Terry and Wolf would have wanted."

*More than 10,000 people turned out to watch the Bishop brothers' final trip down Stratford Broadway. The mourners, lining the route from the undertakers William Denys to St John's Church, were an odd mix of heavy metal fans, everyday East Enders, trade unionists, West Ham hooligans, soap actors, boxers and sportsmen, local politicians and burly men in black suits and dark glasses with too much jewellery. With police keeping a discreet distance, the Iron Army in black leather jackets cleared a path from the chapel of rest to the horse drawn coaches in which the Bishop brothers' coffins were to be carried. The wreaths, including ones from Barbara Windsor and Angry Anderson, could have filled Upton Park. In her speech at the chapel, widow Sylvia Bishop told the assembled mourners that the brothers had performed "a mythical service in a rapidly changing England, providing a sense of glamour and identity, and showing that working class kids with nothing but talent could still make their mark on the world".

*'Harder Than The Rest', Sylvie's official biography of Iron Hammer, topped the best-seller lists in five countries and was turned into an award-winning feature film.

*A Scotland Yard investigation into corruption in various East London police stations including Canning Town and Stratford led to twelve arrests; five other officers took early retirement.

*Victoria Boosler was promoted internally to a more senior role in MI5's counter-proliferation branch.

*Jennifer Evison became a member of the Nigel Lythgoe Dancers and could often be seen on ITV variety shows throughout the 90s.

*DS Dan Roberts was so traumatised by the deaths of his fellow officers that he turned to comfort eating and piled on three stone. He was eighteen stone when he was pictured falling flat on his back as he failed to apprehend a drunken footballer on a bender. The *Daily Star* ran the photo on their front page along with the headline, Scotland Lard.

*Tricia Hodges stood as a Conservative parliamentary candidate for Vauxhall in 1992. She lost but married her campaign manager, Charlie Booker who made his fortunes from derivatives after the Big Bang.

*The phone call from Stratford Police Station to Terry Bishop in the upstairs office of the Athena Apollo was traced directly to the desk of DC Tony Wilson – the same Tony Wilson who had called in sick on the night that DC Tony

Durrant and DC Nick Wells were murdered. DC Wilson was an immediate past master of the Royal Boleyn Masonic Lodge whose other officers included Terence Bishop and Chad Matthews. Four other members of the lodge were police officers. All were arrested and, after Tony Wilson's testimony, all were charged with perverting the course of justice and found guilty.

*The extent of criminal liaisons with corrupt officers in East London led to the launch of the top-secret Operation Othona – known as the Ghost Squad – in 1993. The covert anti-corruption investigation worked separately from other Met detective squads. Most of the records from the operation and their findings were deliberately shredded in the early noughties.

*Mark 'Plumstead' Corrigan, Chad, Spider and Psycho Manny served eight-year sentences for firearm offences. Tesco Eddie, who was unarmed, served four years. After their release, Chad went on to become a successful dancehall DJ, and Plumstead operated a three-card monte team and other street scams in Soho. Spider Jeffries was arrested three years later for a people smuggling racket. He hanged himself on remand. Tesco Eddie went upmarket and got a job at Waitrose. Psycho Manny worked the doors with Dave Courtney, married an heiress and, over time, grew slightly less angry. He has even been known to smile.

*One-Gin Denny walked away with a suspended sentence for possession. He became a jobbing actor appearing in EastEnders and The Bill.

*Henry Gibson became a multimillionaire through his continued successful management of Iron Hammer, who went on to hit triple platinum status in the United States and to sell twelve million albums in South America alone. His management company was based offshore. His co-directors were Steven and Kenneth Knight.

Glossary of Slang Terms

Ag – trouble, short for aggravation

Apples - £20 notes (rhyming slang; apple cores = scores)

April – tool (rhyming slang; April Fool = tool = weapon)

Arthur – hard man (rhyming slang Arthur Mullard = hard; archaic).

Aris – arse (rhyming slang; Aristotle = bottle, bottle and glass = arse; see Queen Mum)

Bacon Bonce – child molester (rhyming slang, bacon bonce = nonce)

Bag – £1,000 (rhyming slang, bang of sand = grand)

Banged up – imprisoned

Bang to rights – caught red-handed; guilty

Barry – a big woman (rhyming slang, Barry McGuigan = a big'un)

Battle-cruiser – pub (rhyming slang, boozer)

Bent – Crooked or stolen goods

Bent – gay (see iron)

Beer tokens – pounds sterling (see sov)

Betty – Table (rhyming slang, Betty Gable = table)

Billies – punters (rhyming slang, Billy Bunters = punters).

Billy – amphetamines (slang from the cartoon character, Billy Whizz)

Bird – time in prison (bird lime = time)

Blade-runner – someone transporting stolen goods.

Blag – to rob, originally a pay-roll or money delivery in a public place.

Blagger – a robber

Boat – face (boat race = face; see also Chevvy Chase).

Bob Hope – cannabis (rhyming slang, Bob Hope = dope; see also puff)

The boob – prison.

To boost – to hot-wire a car.

Boracic – skint (rhyming slang, boracic lint = skint).

Bottle out – to lose one's nerve (see brick it).

Brass – prostitute (see also Tom, dripper)

Brick it – to bottle out.

Britney Spears – ears

Bromleys – toes (rhyming slang, Bromley-by-Bows = toes)

Brown bread – dead (rhyming slang)

A bullseye - £50

A bung – a bribe

Bushel – neck (rhyming slang, bushel and peck; see also Gregory)

Butchers – a look (Butcher's Hook, rhyming slang)

Caked – wealthy (also cake-o, from the expression a cake of notes)

Canister – head (see Swede)

Carpet – three months imprisonment

Cash and Carry, commit – suicide (rhyming slang, hari-kari)

Charlie – cocaine, see also Chas, sherbet, marching powder, nose-bag, Gianluca, Ying, gear, King Lear, Dave's mate).

Chavvy – a child (Romany)

China – mate (rhyming slang, china plate).

Chiv – a knife.

The Church – Customs & Excise (C of E)

Clean – innocent.

Clobber – clothes (see also schmutta)

Cobblers – rubbish (rhyming slang, cobblers' awls = balls)

A cockle – £10 (rhyming slang, cockle and hen = ten).

Collar felt – to be arrested, as in "He had his collar felt")

The Currant – The *Sun* newspaper (rhyming slang, currant bun)

Dabs – finger prints.

Daisy – a safe-breaking tool

Darby – belly (rhyming slang, Darby Kelly = belly; see also Darby Kell)

Dave's mate – cocaine, from Chas and Dave, as used in the phrase "Is Dave's mate about tonight?"

Dipper – a pick pocket.

The dog – the telephone (rhyming slang, dog and bone).

Doris – a woman.

Dot – rotten (rhyming slang, Dot Cotton = rotten), as in "It's all gone Dot Cotton).

A drink – a bribe, ranging from a drink to a nice drink to a handsome drink.

Dripper – see brass.

Drumming – house-breaking.

Dustbins – children (rhyming slang, dustbin lids = kids)

An earner – easy money.

Elephants – drunk (rhyming slang, elephants trunk = drunk; see also Brahms, from Brahms & Liszt = pissed; all archaic)

Eyetie – Italian

Feds – the police

Fence – a receiver of stolen goods

The Filth – the police (see also Old Bill, cossers, rozzers, Plod, Feds, bogeys)

Firm – a gang

To fit-up – to give or plant false evidence.

Flowery – cell (rhyming slang, Flowery dell = cell)

Forsyte's – lager (rhyming slang, Forsyte Saga = lager)

Four-be – a Jew (rhyming slang, 4 be 2)

In the frame – to be the prime suspect.

Frankie – cut-throat razor (rhyming slang, Frankie Fraser)

A friend of ours – one of us. A friend of mine, means he seems OK but hasn't been fully referenced.

Gaff – a house, see also drum and gaff of a gaff (a mansion)

The Game – prostitution, as in on the game

Garrity (to go Garrity) – to go mad, an expression inspired by the sixties pop star Freddie Garrity who fronted Freddie & The Dreamers

Gary – toilet or anus (rhyming slang, Gary Glitter = shitter)

George Young – tongue (rhyming slang)

Gianluca – cocaine (Gianluca Vialli = Charlie)

Gillian = blow job (from Gillian Taylforth; see also a large G&T)

To give a pull – to impart words of advice.

Goldfish, to slip her the goldfish – sex (see pogger)

Gold watch – Scotch (rhyming slang)

Graft – work, or piece of villainy

A grass – an informer.

Gregory – neck (rhyming slang, Gregory Peck)

Grumble – vagina (rhyming slang, grumble & grunt = cunt)

Gypsy's – a piss (rhyming slang, Gypsy's kiss; see also slash, lash, leak and Jimmy)

Half-chat – mixed race

Hampton – penis (rhyming slang, Hampton wick = prick)

Hand Grenades – AIDS (rhyming slang)

Hank Marvin – starving (rhyming slang).

Harry – semen (rhyming slang, Harry Monk = spunk)

A Henry – an eighth of an ounce of cannabis, from Henry VIII

An ice cream – a man/geezer (rhyming slang, ice cream freezer).

Irish – wig (rhyming slang, Irish jig = wig; see also Syrup)

Iron – gay man (rhyming slang, iron hoof = poof).

On your Jack – alone (rhyming slang, Jack Jones; also on your Tod, from Tod Sloan).

Jack and Danny – vagina (rhyming slang, fanny)

Jack The Ripper – stripper (rhyming slang)

Jacks - £5 (rhyming slang, Jack's Alive)

Jacksie – arse.

Jamjar – car (rhyming slang)

Jam Tart – heart (rhyming sland)

A Janet – a quarter of an ounce of cannabis (rhyming slang, Janet Street-Porter = quarter)

Jekyll – fake (Jekyll & Hide = snide)

Jiggle – someone French (rhyming slang, jiggle and jog = frog)

Jimmy – urinate (rhyming slang, Jimmy Riddle = piddle; see also Gypsy's).

Jimmies – lungs (rhyming slang, Jimmy Youngs = lungs)

Jivvle – a woman (dismissive term)

Joe – a Pakistani (rhyming slang, Joe Daki)

Johnny Vaughan – porn (rhyming slang)

K - £1,000.

K – Ketamine (also Special K)

Kate – army (rhyming slang, Kate Karney = army)

Khazi – toilet (see Gary).

Khyber – arse (rhyming slang, Khyber Pass)

A Kim Jong-un – a wrong'un

Kosher – the real thing.

A long firm – a business set up and allowed to run over a fairly lengthy period with the sole intention of defrauding creditors.

On the lash – enjoying a drinking session

Mangled – drunk (see also Elephants; Elephant's Trunk = drunk)

Manor – neighbourhood

To mark yer cards – to give advice.

Minces – eyes (rhyming slang, mince pies)

A monkey – £500.

Moody – fake.

A mug – a stupid person (also Muppet).

To mulla – to beat up.

Mutton – deaf (rhyming slang, Mutt and Jeff = deaf)

Ned – TV (rhyming slang, Ned Kelly = telly)

Nigerian Lager – Guinness.

A nonce – child sex offender.

North and south – (rhyming slang, mouth)

Nugget – a £1 coin

Oedipus – sex (rhyming slang, Oedipus Rex = sex; archaic' see pogger)

Oily – cigarette (rhyming slang, oily rag = fag)

OP – observation post

Orchestras – testicles (rhyming slang, orchestra stalls = balls; see also cobbler's awls)

A parcel – a consignment of stolen goods.

Patsies – piles (rhyming slang, Patsy Palmers = Farmers, Farmer Giles = piles)

Pet the poodle – female masturbation (also beat the beaver, hit the slit, juice the sluice, bash the gash, slam the clam)

A Peter – a safe.

Pete Tong – wrong (rhyming slang)

Pigs – beer (rhyming slang, pig's ear = beer, usually on George Raft – draft)

Plates – feet (rhyming slang, plates of meat)

Pogger – to make love to, aggressively, as in 'I poggered the granny out of her'

A pony - £25 (also macaroni).

Pony – rubbish (rhyming slang, pony and trap = crap)

Pop – to pawn (rhyming slang, popcorn = pawn)

Porkies – lies (rhyming slang, porky pie).

Puff – cannabis (also dope, Bob Hope, grass, blow, wacky baccy, ganja, weed, Beryl Reid, pot, the magic dragon).

Pukka – authentic (see Ream).

Queen Mum – the anus (rhyming slang, Queen Mum = bum; see Aris)

Rabbit – talk (rhyming slang, rabbit and pork = talk; see also bunny)

Raspberry – disabled person (rhyming slang, raspberry ripple – cripple)

Rattle – bank (rhyming slang, rattle and clank = bank)

Ream – the real thing, or of good quality (see Pukka)

On the Rock 'n' Roll – unemployed (rhyming slang, rock 'n' roll = dole)

Rosy – tea (rhyming slang, Rosy Lee)

Rubber – pub (rhyming slang, rub-a-dub; see also battle cruiser = boozer)

Ruby – curry (rhyming slang, Ruby Murray = curry).

Salmon – erection (rhyming slang, salmon and prawn = horn; also lob-on)

Saucepan – child (rhyming slang, saucepan lid = kid)

Schnide – fake (see also Sexton Blake)

Score - £20 (see apple).

See You Next Tuesday – a cunt

Septic – an American (rhyming slang, Septic Tank = yank)

Sexton Blake – counterfeit goods (rhyming slang, Sexton Blake - fake)

A sherbet – a cab (rhyming slang, sherbet dab)

Shovel – jail (rhyming slang, shovel and pail = jail; see also the can, clink, chokey, the pen, the hole)

Silvery – a black man (rhyming slang, silvery spoon; see also Feargal Sharkey)

Skin and blister – sister (rhyming slang)

Slag – a person with no principles.

Slaphead – a bald man, one who wears the pink crash helmet

A slaughter – a safe place to dispose of stolen goods, short for slaughter-house.

Smack – heroin (also horse, H, junk, skag, shit, brown, Harry, the white palace, the Chinaman's nightcap.)

A smudger – a photographer

Sniffer – a reporter (rhyming slang, sniffers and snorters = reporters)

The Spanish Archer – the sack (Spanish archer = El Bow; see also tin-tack = sack)

A sov - £1, from sovereign.

SP – information, from starting prices.

Speed – amphetamines (see Billy)

Spiel – patter.

Squirt – ammonia in a bottle.

A steward's – an investigation, from steward's inquiry.

A stretch – one year in prison.

Strides – trousers

Stripe – to cut the face with a Frankie or a chiv

Surrey Docks – syphilis (rhyming slang, Surrey Docks = Pox)

Swagman – a dealer in cheap goods

Swede – head (see canister)

A syrup – wig (rhyming slang, syrup of figs)

Taters – cold (rhyming slang, taters in the mould; also brass monkeys from 'it's cold enough to freeze the balls off a brass monkey).

Tea-leaf – thief (rhyming slang)

Thrupennies – breasts (rhyming slang, thruppenny bits – tits; see also Earthas, Eartha Kitts, and Bristols, Bristol Cities – titties)

Tiddlies – Chinese people (rhyming slang, tiddly wink = chink)

Tin-Tack – sack (rhyming slang, tin-tack = sack; see also the Spanish Archer – El Bow).

Tits up – to go wrong or pear-shaped.

Tod – alone (rhyming slang, Tod Sloan = alone; see also Jack)

Tom – jewellery (rhyming slang, tomfoolery)

Tom – defecate (rhyming slang, Tom Tit = shit; see also a Forrest, Forrest Gump = dump)

Tool – a weapon (see April)

Top – kill

Turtles – gloves (rhyming slang, turtle doves = gloves)

VAT – vodka and tonic.

Vera – gin (rhyming slang, Vera Lynn = gin)

Weasel – coat (rhyming slang, weasel and stoat = coat)

A whistle – suit (rhyming slang, whistle and flute = suit)

Wipe his mouth – to put up with the situation.

A Wrong'un – a bad or untrustworthy person.

Wutherings – tights (rhyming slang, Wuthering Heights)

A Yard – £1billion (trader slang, half a yard = £500million

Enjoyed **Harder Than The Rest**? Read more of Harry Tyler's adventures in **Face Down**.

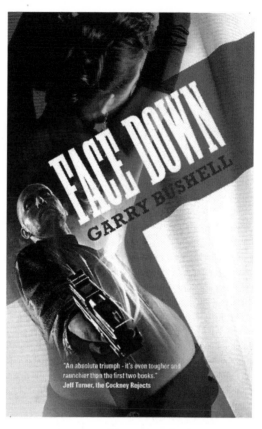

When an angry vigilante takes the law into his own hands the Kent police are stumped. But could the brutal serial killer be taking his cues from an outspoken right wing newspaper columnist? Jailed South London crime lord Johnny Too agrees to be the bait to lure him into the open and end his reign of murder and terror. There's just one problem – he wants retired undercover detective Harry Tyler, the man who put him away, to be part of the plot. And Harry's dead. Isn't he?

Discover more about 1960s Mod villain Steve Knight in All Or Nothing.

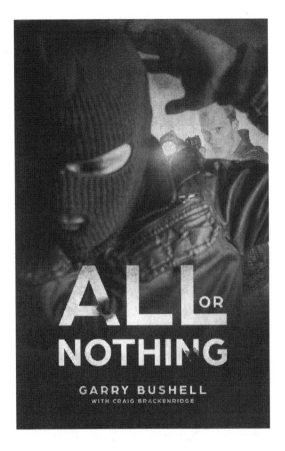

London 1966. The Swinging City, awash with youthful creativity, music and fashion, excitement and opportunity. For men like Steve Knight an East End Mod with a small gang and a big dream.

Steve is smart enough but is he hard enough to see it through? And as the violence escalates, only one thing is certain: not all of them will make it through alive.

Chapter One: The Lion & The Elephant

It was 1966, a dull and wet Saturday afternoon in Hoxton, the historic core of London's East End. A dark blue Commer van sat stationary in a side street, decrepit and uninviting like an ugly aging toad. You wouldn't ordinarily look twice at such a rusting pile of junk. But, if by chance you did, you would probably assume the men inside were building workers, or maybe road diggers on a tea break. Copies of the *Daily Mirror*, the *Daily Express* and *The Sun* adorned the dashboard, along with a couple of thermos flasks and a large white paper bag full of cheese and pickle rolls.

Look a little harder you might also notice that the newspapers weren't being read, the food was not being eaten, the tea remained un-poured, and some of the crew were far too well-dressed to be digging roads.

Sitting directly behind the passenger seat was Steven Harold Knight, a 22-year-old with a passing resemblance to Steve Marriott from the Small Faces. He had the same haircut, but was six inches taller, broader and looked considerably stronger than the diminutive Cockney rocker. Like a million other men his age, Steve Knight was a mod. But not many of them could afford the Girard-Perregaux Automatic Silver Dial watch he wore so casually on his left wrist or his obsessively polished hand-stitched Chelsea boots.

The transistor radio on the dashboard was playing "With a Girl Like You" by the Troggs but Knight wasn't listening to it. He was lost deep in his own thoughts...

Respect. That was what today was all about. Knowing your place. Knowing who was top dog. Not taking liberties...It was a day to settle scores and not just on a certain hallowed turf thirteen miles away via the North Circular.

Without thinking Steve used his right thumb to tap each of the fingers on his right hand: *1-2-3-4, 1-2-3-4, 1-2-3-4, 1-2-3-4...*

On the radio "Black Is Black" by Los Bravos had taken over from Reg Presley. Steve glanced around the freshly stolen van's dingy interior.

There was a smell of diesel and paint from inside the vehicle and another unmistakeable scent – not of fear as such, more like nervous anticipation. Time to lighten the mood...

'Turn that shit off, Kenny.'

His brother duly obliged.

'Right, so this lion is chasing this rabbit,' Steve said in an accent so Cockney it could have been scraped off the counter of Tubby Isaac's eel stall. 'It goes down an 'ole and as the lion tries to follow it, 'e gets jammed. Now the lion's stuffed. He can't move his 'ead and his jacksie is stuck up in the air wavin' about. An' this elephant wanders past and thinks *why not?*'

Everyone in the van was now smiling. 'So bosh' – *BOSSSH!* – "e gives the lion a quick one up the khyber. Well the lion don't like it, does 'e, and he starts wriggling and struggling and jerkin' about until finally 'e pulls 'is nut out of the rabbit hole. He's got the right 'ump, this lion, and 'e chases after the elephant. The elephant legs it into an expedition tent, where he sees a pith helmet and a copy of the *Sunday Express*. 'E puts on the 'elmet an' 'olds the paper in front of his boat. This lion charges in and roars "Oi mate, have you seen an elephant in here?" The elephant lowers the newspaper and says "You mean the one that fucked you up the arse?" The lion says "What? it's made the paper already?"...'

The van exploded in laughter.

'Bit later the 'unter, whose tent it was, goes to the doctor complaining of a sore arse. The doc examines 'im and says "My God, how did your arsehole get so stretched?" The hunter says "I got fucked by an elephant." The doctor says "There's a lot of that about. But 'old on, everyone knows elephant dicks are long but they ain't *that* wide." The hunter shrugs and says: "He stuck his finger in first".'

Now the men were in fits. The loudest guffaws came from the Spicer brothers, a pair of keen, thin-faced young middleweight boxers from the manor. They were good lads, Steve thought, and always happy to turn a blind eye to the Marquees of Queensberry's rule book whenever there was a decent drink in it. Like today.

The Spicers were bobbing about impatiently up front with Kenny, who was sitting across from Steve in the driving seat chewing so loudly on a stick of gum that it echoed across the metal roof.

Wrigley's had a slogan: Sealed Tight, Kept Right. That was just how this firm ought to be, Steve thought. It wasn't. Not yet. But it would be.

In the back of the nondescript van were Vic Naboth, Pat McVey, Matty Beeston and Roy Storer – the inner core of the Knight gang – plus Mo, Curly and Larry, three trusted older geezers known collectively as the "Three Stooges", who they had roped in for this afternoon's fun and games.

It was quite a team, but not one that Steve was entirely happy with.

He and Kenny had inherited the firm after their old man copped it. They weren't hand-picked. Apart from his oldest friend Roy, who he'd recruited personally, this lot had been passed down to him like family heirlooms. They'd had value once, but had been knocked about a bit. They were damaged goods.

He'd had this very discussion with Kenny earlier in the week. His brother didn't seem to mind, but Steve had a bolder vision. He wanted fresh blood, a whole firm in their 20s, just like the two of them.

Spank out the old, slam in the new!

Society was changing fast and with a new decade less than four years away he knew the whole crew had to be as dynamic and opportunistic as he was.

Most of the current mob had barely changed their hairstyles since they were demobbed.

With his hair gel, quiff, sideburns and ducktail barnet, Patrick McVey looked every bit the 1950s throwback. The Monday Club was less resistant to change. Pat, also known as "Mad Pat" was useful though. He was a big man with a short fuse and a cleft chin of solid granite; unshaven, with a stare that could strip wallpaper and a face like a clenched fist.

The sort of bloke who would give a bad dream nightmares. "Hulking" was probably the adjective that summed him up best.

Kenny looked at his watch. 'Half-time just ended.'

Steve nodded. 'Give it a few minutes.'

As they sat in silence, McVey reached inside his donkey jacket, pulled out a heavy Colt M1917 revolver and gave it the once-over.

'Do us a favour, Pat,' chortled Roy. 'Where did you get that fuckin' thing? Was "Wild Bill" Hickok having a closing down sale, mate?'

'What else are you packing, Patrick?' asked Matty. 'A blunderbuss? A cutlass stuck down yer almond?'

'Nah, he keeps that in his pantaloons.'

'Cheeky cunts,' snarled Pat. 'It'll do the fucking job, that's what counts, ain't it?'

He flashed two nicotine stained fingers at his detractors. Steve looked over at the three men and raised his eyebrows at Roy. 'I have to say Pat, it ain't gonna do much for our image, mate.'

'Fuck that, by the time they see it they'll be too busy wondering where their kneecaps went to pass comment.'

Pat jammed the gun back into his waistband under his jacket and out of sight.

'I make him right,' said Kenny. 'I don't care what we hit these bastards with as long as they get hit...hard. Our old man put up with these fuckers for too long and now they're taking the piss. If they think they can fuck with us up West then they need a reminder about who is in charge.'

Pat lit a Woodbine. Steve shook his head. Even his fags were out of time. Sighing inwardly he slipped his hand into the right pocket of his black Italian-cut suit. It was a year old but it still looked the business. There was a card in the pocket which he absent-mindedly caressed four times before taking it out. It was a business card bearing the legend Bernard Sternschuss, Diamond Trader, also known as 'Bernie the fence'.

That reminded him, the last time he'd worn this whistle had been at his father's funeral...

'I wonder what the score is?' said Matty, drumming his fingers impatiently. 'Can't we listen to the game on the radio for a bit?'

'Fuck the score,' Kenny snorted. 'Those Jock bastards are probably all in there, waving their little Kraut flags.'

'Yep, that's the point,' said Steve. 'While the Sweaty mugs are all glued to the box getting lathered, watching our boys kick a fucking Slazenger Challenge ball about with the Hun, none of them will be expecting company.'

'It's unpatriotic, that's what it is. Working on a day like this.'

'Shut the fuck up, Matt,' Kenny snapped. 'Just make sure you're ready for this or you'll never see Bobby Moore again. Ever! These bastards won't fuck about.'

Steve nodded. Kenny was right, the McCaffertys were a serious firm. But they had to deliver the message so clearly that a pair of pig-thick Sweaty cow-sons could get it. As of today, they were out of the uppers trade for good.

It was mod that had made the McCaffertys a problem. The gang were a loose collection of exiled Scots who operated out of a spit-and-sawdust boozer on Southgate Road in Hoxton. Barry and Iain "Tug" McCafferty had fled Glasgow in the late 1950s when they fell out of favour with Jock MacDonald, a mobster located in the north of the city. They ended up in the relative safety of the New North Road, a goal kick or two away from Shoreditch Park, and immediately started getting their fingers dirty in whatever murky business they could find.

Arrogant and brutal, the McCaffertys paid scant regard to the firms already operating in the area, and multiple confrontations ensued.

Many ended violently. The Jocks were ruthless bastards with their liberal use of cut-throat razors, the word rapidly got around – avoid this pair like the plague.

A dozen or so victims still walked the streets of London N1 bearing the slash marks of the brothers' "malky" – "Malky Fraser" being Glaswegian slang for "razor". They were a living reminder that messing with the McCaffertys was not good for your skincare regime.

As the new decade dawned the brothers chanced upon the amphetamines market. It had started small-scale but in '62, in Tug's words, it "'took off like Johnnie Johnson' as London's early urban mod elite spawned a mainstream, nationwide cult.

Mod fashion was the new cool and even kids in suburbia were into looking sharp and buzzing about on Vespas and Lambrettas.

"Little pills" officially known as Drinamyl were a vital component of the scene, dished out by quacks to bored housewives, depressive types and greedy bastards who needed to lose weight. These uppers gave users energy and drive.

Amphetamines powered the whole mod underground and were available in different forms. But whether they were French blues, black bombers, black and white minstrels or purple hearts – which were neither purple nor heart-shaped – the kids gobbled them up by the handful to make sure that there was never any chance of letting sleep get in the way of a good time.

The teenage "tickets" had no need of Morpheus, they were already living the dream.

By 1964, business was properly booming and the McCaffertys saw no reason to limit their operation to neighbouring Islington, Highbury and Canonbury. Mickey Knight had warned the brothers not to step on his toes by flogging their whizz on his patch up West but, although they'd agreed to his face, the bastards continued to take liberties and, for some reason, Steven never understood why his father always failed to take action.

That had to stop.

With their old man out of the picture, the Knights knew they had to make a clear statement of intent. The McCaffertys had been a boil on their necks for too long. Putting the Jocks back in their box would show the world that they were in charge and would no longer tolerate dissent from anyone on or around their empire. The "Scottish problem" was about to come MacScreaming to an abrupt full stop.

***

The streets outside The Jolly Farmer were remarkably tranquil for a late Saturday afternoon – unsurprising given the importance of the game at Wembley Stadium that was holding England's attention. It was the perfect opportunity to strike the McCaffertys at their most unguarded, the Knights had decided, and nothing short of total victory would do.

'It was like 'Flodden or Culloden re-played on home turf,' Steve had said last night.

'What's soddin' "Floddin" when it's at 'ome?' Ken, who read less, had replied.

'It's still quiet out there,' Kenny said softly as he peered through the windscreen and looked up and down the street. 'It's got to be time now, Steven.'

His brother nodded.

'All right lads. Hands off cocks, hands on tools and whatever else you need, this is it.'

The tension inside the van thickened like the London smog as the mob tightened their grips on the array of weapons which they had brought along. It was an eclectic mix of chains, hatchets, clubs and coshes; plus Mad Pat McVey's antique firearm.

'You know the drill,' Steve continued urgently. 'Hit whoever is nearest and if any gutless wonder has it on their toes then let 'em go. Leave the brothers to me and Kenny. Don't hold back though, anyone who stands alongside those Jock cunts deserves what they get.'

'Yes, sir,' muttered McVey in a half-whisper that was meant to be heard.

Steve smiled but his eyes registered minus ten degrees Fahrenheit. Pat's tone, his manner, his irritating fucking presence, made Steve want to beat his fat, Neanderthal face until his knuckles bled. Instead he took a deep breath and tapped the leather cosh in his hand against his leg four times. 1-2-3-4.

***

The Knight firm burst into the pub like an Atlantic storm. The dozen or so men inside were so entranced watching the football action on the small Perdio Portarama TV set perched up on the bar that it took a few moments for them to register that they were under attack. Barry McCafferty was closest to the door and Kenny took him out of the picture with a single swing of an iron bar. Barry fell badly and landed face down on the floor with his arm hanging loosely over an upturned bar stool. Kenny drove his weapon down heavily on the exposed limb and a sickening crack echoed above the escalating din.

Pat McVey's rusty pistol banged loudly twice and someone dropped to the floor with a flood of claret spreading across his trousers just above the knee. Pat fired again but the gun clicked impotently so he slammed the heavy weapon straight into the face of an oncoming foe, shattering his nose.

Pandemonium broke out as the Knight firm laid into punter after punter with punishing blows. A few "big jessies" legged it, but for the most part the McCaffertys' mob were a game bunch. Most of them chose fight over flight. Knives, clubs and razors were out in an instant and being put to work on the invaders. Preparation, coupled with the element of surprise, worked well in the Knight gang's favour however and the McCafferty cronies were soon leaving crimson patches on the pub's worn wooden floor.

Steve went straight for Tug, the older and most feared of the two brothers. He lashed out with his cosh but the red-faced Scotsman ducked surprisingly sharply and drove a meaty fist deep into Steve's guts.

Every ounce of breath exploded from Steve's lungs and as he bent over gasping for air Tug brought his knee straight up into his jaw. *THWACK!* Then his right arm curled around his neck and tightened into a headlock. Steve struggled, his lungs battled desperately for oxygen, his heart rate rocketed, his eyes stung with sweat. Tug increased the pressure. The room span, and everything drifted out of focus. The void beckoned.

Steve heard his name being shouted and there was a dull thud as Tug McCafferty fell to the ground beside him. The back of his head missed a four-inch shard of broken glass by less than an inch. Roy Storer had crowned "King Jock" with a billy club.

Steve fell too, gasping frantically for air as a sea of boots threatened to engulf them both. The whole room was locked in brutal combat. Steve used the last ounce of his strength to roll on top of Tug and push his fingers around the Jock's throat.

'Yer old man is long deid, Knight, and it's just business as usual for us,' hissed Tug as he struggled to loosen Steve's grip around his windpipe.

'It's not business as usual, you cunt. For you it ain't even business any more,' snarled Steve. 'If you even sell so much as an aspirin between Marylebone and the Embankment you'll be going back to *Glasgae* in a fuckin' wooden box.'

Deep within Tug's eyes Steve saw a flicker of defiance. He needed a final flourish to hammer his message home. The shard of glass was still in reach. Steve grabbed it up and dug it hard into Tug's cheekbone before dragging it down to the edge of his mouth, scarring the Jock the way that he liked to scar his victims.

Tug McCafferty gave a kind of gurgled scream. The glass cut deeply into Steve's fingers too, but he ignored the pain and kept going until the three-inch gash was complete. Tug writhed on the floor, cupping the wound with both hands. His blood was pouring through the gaps in his fingers.

Gulping the air greedily, Steve struggled to his feet. He could feel his own blood dripping from his fingers like warm milk, but the sight of Tug writhing on the ground gave him a rush of adrenalin that washed away the discomfort. He threw back his head and gave a primal roar then slammed the heel of his boot down on the Scotsman's groin.

Still dazed, Steve looked around. The McCaffertys' mob were far from done. They were going toe to toe and tool to tool against his gang. Matty was down but everyone else was still standing, though bald Curly was bleeding heavily from a deep cut above his left ear.

A ginger giant resembling an over-sized, partially shaved Yeti was writhing in agony on the pub floor. His legs were twisted like liquorice but Roy was still smashing away at his knee caps like an angry convict breaking rocks in the hot sun with a sledgehammer.

To his immediate right Steve saw Kenny and Rab Buchan, one of the McCafferty's cousins, rolling apart violently on the floor. The young Jock lashed out at his brother's left leg with a Stanley knife, tearing his Harry Fenton strides but barely cutting his flesh. Kenny clamped down on his wrist with his right hand and slammed Rab's head hard against the floorboard. This stunned him for the moment it took Kenny to roll on top of him and press his own blade against his throat. 'That's you brown bread, son,' he snarled, before knocking him spark out with a clean left.

All three of the McCafferty's top boys were out of the game.

Steve roared and re-joined the fray, smashing into anyone who stood between him and his firm. 'Back! Back!' one of the Jocks hollered as those of them still standing retreated and regrouped in a defensive semi-circle at the other end of the bar.

Steve snarled at them. 'You tell Pinky and Perky 'ere when they come round that if they give us any more shit, the next time we come back none of youse will get out alive.'

He helped Matty up from the deck and supported him as the Knight firm backed out slowly into the street. Inside the pub an eerie quiet descended. Over the groaning of the injured there was only the muffled sound of the TV which had been knocked off the bar in the melee and was now lodged in the sink behind the jump.

'Some people are on the pitch!' it boomed. 'They think it's all over! It is now...!'

***

Kenny and Steve had been up to mischief as long as they could remember. When their mother died giving birth to Steve, their dear old Auntie Eth had tried the best she could to steer them onto the straight and narrow but, with an old man like Mickey Knight, she was pissing in the wind without a brolly. The boys were still in short trousers when they started helping their dad unload hijacked trucks and deliver dodgy packages around the backstreets of Shoreditch.

Steve was a clever kid, much smarter than his father. He could have gone to grammar school, his teachers wanted him to, and so did Auntie Eth. But Steve insisted on going to the local secondary modern like Kenny had. It was where all his mates were going.

By the time he was thirteen, the brothers had graduated to liaising with Fred Prevost, a shop steward in Albert Dock whose network of dockers maintained a constant supply of stolen goods, mostly spirits and clothing. They sold and consumed some of the hooky gear themselves, but were more than happy to flog the bulk of it on via the Knight Organisation distribution network – KO'd if you crossed them.

A little later, he and Kenny were collecting the odd chunk of protection money and occasionally delivering bricks through the windows of some of Mickey's debtors. Once he had started shaving, school was elbowed and the boys entered the family business full-time.

They were a handsome pair of lads with a trail of broken hearts to prove it. Granted Kenny had a touch of the Henry Cooper about him, but Steve's matinee idol looks were responsible for more moist gussets than Adam Faith. When Mickey's business expanded into the West End in the early 1960s staying well clear of the Krays operations in Knightsbridge – the lads were in their prime, never less than immaculately dressed and always with that type of ready cash that attracted the crumpet, young and old.

After Mickey's unexpected demise last year, no one expected the boys to step up and continue the family business. That they had done so, with a vicious relish, silenced most of their doubters and detractors. But not all of them.

In the aftermath of the attack on the McCaffertys, Steve and Kenny had laid low for a few days in case of repercussions. None came and within a week they were back in action as a visible presence. The brothers made a priority of visiting all of the establishments which paid for their "services". The message got around quickly. It was business as usual.

Rumour had it that Tug and Barry McCafferty had been patched up and caught the next available bus back to bonny Jockland. The word through the grapevine was that their pub in Hoxton was still in a bad state of repair and was doing very little business. The Knights had achieved the desired effect but it had been a close run thing. Steve knew that if they were to avoid a similar outcome in the future then they needed to stack the odds more heavily in their favour. Vic and Matty were knocking on, and approaching retirement age, and although Mad Pat McVey was up to full match fitness his behaviour was becoming increasingly erratic.

The big man had never really accepted Kenny and Steve as Mickey's successors and was not shy of airing these views in public.

This needed sorting. Fast.

***

Pat McVey sauntered into the Dover Castle just as Chris Farlowe's "Out Of Time" started up on the Rock-Ola jukebox. *You're obsolete my baby...* Apt, thought Steve Knight. Very fucking apt.

'Turn that shite off,' Pat barked at Eric the barman, and then laughed when the little guy meekly ran straight over and unplugged the machine.

It was a Wednesday night but the boozer was deserted, save for Steve, Kenny, Matty, Vic and Roy who were plotting up around a table at the back of the room. Eric nodded respectfully at Pat before bolting the front door and disappearing out the back.

Around twenty bottles of ales – Mann's Brown, Bass Pale and Banks's Mild – sat on the bar next to a bottle of Johnnie Walker Red Label whisky and some glasses.

'Get yourself a sherbert, Patrick, and join us,' said Kenny with a welcoming smile.

'It's a closed shop tonight then, is it?' said Pat as he poured himself a large measure of Scotch and casually glanced back at the door.

'Just a bit of discreet business tonight, mate,' said Steve. 'I'm sure the local pissheads can survive for one evening.'

McVey grunted and glugged down some whisky before he plodded over to join the group. Steve surveyed him like a professional poker player eyeing up his hand. Pat was the hardest of them all, and also the hardest to like. Thickset and unkempt, McVey had an air of repressed violence about him that was never far from the surface.

Even his clothes bore a grudge.

The big man dropped down heavily onto a seat. Up close his face looked like badly laid crazy paving, a mess of scars – some from acne, some from knives and broken bottles.

'Did you hear Pat's got himself a new telly?' Matty said mischievously. 'A big old Pye set...'

'How much did that set you back, Pat?' asked Roy.

'Fuck all!' said Vic, laughing. 'He just walked into the shop, picked it up and walked out again. The geezer said "You can't do that" and what did you tell him, Pat?'

'Who's gonna stop me?' McVey said. Everyone chuckled. Then Pat looked directly at the Knights.

'What's this all about then?' he asked abruptly.

'We'd just like to thank you all for the past couple of days,' said Kenny. 'We know you've been busy out and about letting our "clients" know it is business as usual. It's been a rough week but things are going well, so cheers to you all.'

Kenny raised his glass. 'To us!' he said. The others tipped their own drinks towards him. 'To us!' they echoed, all except McVey who only grunted loudly.

'You all right, Pat?' said Steve as he caught McVey's eye.

'Of course...*guv'nor*,' said Pat. Nobody missed the side order of sarcasm that underpinned his reply.

Kenny spoke quickly in an attempt to steamroller a path through the bad atmosphere. 'Things are going well and we thought it might be time for a little expansion, maybe it's time to bring some new blood on board.'

'More fucking boys,' Pat mumbled under his breath.

'You got something to say, Pat?' said Steve sharply. His patience hadn't quite snapped but, like an unmarried mum with no change for the electric meter, it was half an inch away from breaking point. 'We're all ready for your pearls of homespun wisdom.'

McVey glared defiantly across the table. 'Do you think we need back up do you? What's the matter? Has yer bottle gone?'

Steve's complexion coloured but he remained in his seat, upright and staring McVey in the face. 'There's nothing wrong with my bottle, Pat.'

'Oh yeah?' hissed McVey. 'You weren't very lively the other night. Tug McCafferty had you on the deck right away. If it weren't for Roy here he'd have finished you off. You were fucking lucky to put him down.'

Steve was seething inside but he fought to keep a calm demeanour.

'Now come on, Pat,' yelled Kenny. 'You are fucking out of order.'

'You want to take over London but putting a few Jocks out of the picture nearly done you both in,' spat McVey. 'It's all fucking wrong, if your old fella could see you now he'd be pig-sick.'

'You old cunt,' yelled Roy as he leapt across the table and slammed his fist into the side of McVey's head. It wasn't the first punch McVey had received out of the blue and it wouldn't be the last. Although he staggered as he got up from his chair, he instinctively lashed out and caught his attacker squarely on the chin.

Roy fell back against the wall and onto the ground. McVey slid a flick knife from his pocket and clicked it swiftly into life. Steve and Vic pounced on him immediately and restrained him while Kenny grabbed his wrist and roughly shook the blade from his grip.

'You fucking ingrate,' Steve said furiously as he tightened his arm around McVey's neck. 'You'd pull a blade on your own firm? If my dad was 'ere you'd be heading straight down to Limehouse Basin wrapped in tarpaulin. Get the fuck out of 'ere and don't come back until you've sobered up, you psychotic tosspot.'

Vic released his grip on McVey and Steve shoved him towards the door. The big man staggered forward and regained his balance; then he stood his ground defiantly and glared around the bar.

'I'll go,' he snarled. 'But I'm telling you now I won't be fucking back. This firm is going down the crapper and I'm not going with it. There's plenty opportunity for someone with my reputation in this town.'

'Your reputation died out with the ark,' snorted Roy, still nursing his chin.

Steve had regained his composure and was smoothing out the creases in his Anthony Corbett suit jacket as McVey lingered near the door. He looked at him coolly.

'Just go home, Pat, sleep it off,' he said. 'Come back when you're ready.'

'I'm ready now, you flash cunt,' said McVey defiantly. 'I'll go but I'm telling you now, me and Knights, we're fucking finished.'

'Don't be daft, Pat,' said Kenny with a shrug of his shoulders. 'Where are you gunna go? You're one of us.'

'Not any fucking more. You can stick here with Lulu and the Luvvers, Kenny boy, but I'm done.'

McVey left the pub, slamming the door with a bang that echoed around the bar.

'He's a one-off,' said Vic by way of an excuse.

'Thank fuck for that,' sighed Roy.

'He'll be back,' said Matty.

'I don't think so...'

Steve Knight's words stayed suspended ominously in the air like a freshly hanged corpse at Tyburn gallows. No one answered him; no one met his gaze. Vic and Matty dropped their eyes to the floor. The others exchanged glances that ran from triumph to trepidation. For his part Steve attempted to look impassive. He knew Pat of old. He would hit the Scotch and pick fights with random mugs for a few days as he luxuriated in his own fury. And after that, who knew? Patrick McVey wasn't the type to go gently into that good night.

***

It was Steve who remarked that the evening air was 'as cold as Eskimo Nell's outhouse an' just as fuckin' damp', coaxing a grin out of his companions. He pulled the balaclava snugly over his face, grateful for the warmth that it offered. Kenny and Vic did the same. The three men were standing just inside the long tunnel at the end of Wheeler Street that ran beneath the railway line. Roy Storer was just a dark shape in the distance as he stood watch at the other end.

'Who plotted this delivery route?' said Steve suspiciously. 'Have we got a friend in the dispatch office over at the bond?'

'No,' said Kenny. 'They've been using this way for a while now, and have had no trouble. Like I always say, don't fucking strangle the golden goose. We've left them alone for a while so it has left us some nice easy pickings for tonight.'

'Do you still think this is a good idea?' Steve asked quietly.

'You getting cold feet, bruv?'

'No, but McVey was in on this. We don't want him sticking his fucking snout in or grassing us up.'

'Patrick's no rat,' sighed Kenny. 'That's not his style. I think it's a fucking shame. Having a younger firm is all well and good but Dad's old boys are known and respected. Better than that, they're feared. We could always use a human wrecking ball like Pat McVey. There isn't one of us who could have taken him down one on one.'

'He's a fucking dinosaur.'

'Maybe so, bruv, but dinosaurs ran the world for one fuck of a long time. Pat is fearless, and I'm telling you he ain't no grass.'

Steve snorted through the thick black wool that covered his face. 'I wish I could be sure about that. He's always been a wrong'un. He only married Edith coz he wanted a wife to beat.'

Kenny laughed; Vic didn't.

Steve glanced at Naboth. 'Have you seen him?' he asked. The words had an accusatory subtext, like a teacher waiting for a schoolboy to lie about his missing homework.

'Of course I ain't,' Vic replied angrily. 'I don't know where the fuck he is and I don't care.'

Steve grunted. An air of suspicion lingered in the air like a bad smell. Naboth clenched his fists silently in the gloom.

'Look,' said Kenny, 'He's gone and that's all we need to know. Last I heard he was over Millwall way trying to stir up business with some two-bob firm. Everyone knows he's finished round here, now shut the fuck up, I think I can hear something.'

A truck appeared in the distance and they all watched it approach. When it was just a few yards away, Matty emerged from the shadows and unrolled a rubber sheet across the road with a quick flick of his wrist. The thick black strip was embedded with six-inch nails which glistened for a second in the moonlight before the truck rolled right over them. The two front tyres exploded with a hiss and dragged the spiked track along the road before the whole vehicle ground to a shuddering halt against the wall of the tunnel.

There was a loud roar from the engine for a few moments as the throttle gunned wildly and echoed noisily inside the arches. Then it fell silent. All they could hear now was a hiss and some light clinking in the container.

'For fuck's sake,' Steve shouted. 'Talk about over dramatic. There'll be nothing but broken glass left in the back.'

'It did the job, didn't it?' snapped Matty as he ran towards them. 'You wanted it stopped, didn'tcha? Well its fuckin' stopped now.'

'Less fucking chit-chat,' ordered Kenny. Roy ran back through the tunnel towards them and Kenny barked, 'Get the Spicers to bring the van round. Roy, get up front and check out what state the poor cunt is in.'

The Knight brothers strode over to the back of the truck. The unmistakeable oaky smell of single malt livened up the night air.

'Oh, shit,' murmured Kenny. He lifted his bolt cutters up to the heavy padlock that was securing the door. The metal from the shackle clinked loudly as the cutters bit deep, and then the padlock fell onto the spirit-soaked tarmac. Steve pulled one of the doors open to reveal the booty. Result! At least two hundred cases of whisky were strapped to the sides of the container. Only a few had worked loose in the crash and lay shattered on the metal flooring.

Roy and Matty appeared behind the Knights and simultaneously whistled at the surviving stacks of liquid sunshine.

'See, I told you. No problems. The old ways are still the best,' said Matty smugly.

'Piss off,' laughed Roy.

He jumped into the back of the truck with Steve. Both men whipped out large butcher's knives and started to hack away frantically at the straps which held the cases in place. Tony

Spicer backed their stolen van over the grass to the back of the truck then his brother Adrian – "Adey" – jumped out to join the others as they formed a chain to pass the boxes into their vehicle.

Steve kept his eye on the dark, gloomy road behind them as he passed the cases forward. The Old Bill he could handle, but if McVey rolled over the horizon with his new *compadres* then things could get very nasty.

'How's the driver?' said Steve, snapping himself out of his dark thoughts.

'He won't be picking up his pension, let's say that,' said Roy with a streak of gallows humour.

Steve felt a sting of regret. There was no need for that and no need to hurt civilians. He squeezed his left hand with his right four times, taking in a deep breath each time, then continued unloading.

Once they had filled the van, they slammed the back doors closed and ordered the Spicers to drive on to the address they had been given. It was the Knight family slaughterhouse, a small warehouse off Hackney Road which had long been Mickey Knight's safe place to store and divvy up ill-gotten gains.

Before the next day was done the whisky would have been sold on to a network of pubs and clubs...whether they wanted it or not.

Matty and the Spicers clambered into the truck while Kenny, Steve, Vic and Roy followed behind in another car.

The Knights were smart enough never to risk getting stopped by the filth in a truck full of stolen hooch, but the others seemed to neither know, nor care, about the potential consequences.

The road away from the hijack spot was empty, as they had expected it to be at this late hour. Even when they pulled out onto Bethnal Green Road the traffic was light. They stayed a respectable distance away from the truck but only the odd taxi, bin lorry and delivery van were on the road with them.

As they turned off the main drag onto Squirries Street the men noticed the unmistakeable blue light of a police car travelling slowly down the other side of the road towards them.

For a moment time itself seem to slow to a different pace. All of them tensed up but sat stock-still. The cop car decelerated, dropping to the sedate speed of a milk float as it passed the truck. Kenny pushed his head back against the headrest of his seat so that his face was obscured by shadow. Vic, Steve and Roy remained impassive. Heartbeats raced and fingers tightened around tools.

The vehicle slowed down even more as it drew alongside them, they could almost feel the coppers' eyes burning into their faces. *Keep going, keep going, keep going...thank fuck.*

The police car continued on past them, and then suddenly screeched away down the street at speed.

'I think the dozy cunts just heard about the whisky truck,' joked Roy as he expelled a deep breath of relief.

There was a brief giggle from everyone else in the car but Kenny was still watching the cops disappear in the distance. When the car was completely out of sight he whistled loudly and laughed, 'Dozy bastard filth, they couldn't find a cunt in a brothel, fuckin' ars...'

Before he could finish the sentence, a black Zephyr came screaming out of a side street with its headlights on full beam and, shrieking rubber, rammed directly and deliberately straight into them.

The nose of the car hit them right on the driver's side front wheel arch. The Knights' vehicle span with a force that smashed their heads into side windows and left the firm bruised, dazed and disorientated.

In a split second, three young men leapt out of the Zephyr and threw bricks through the car windows which shattered, showering the interior and everyone in it with shards of glass.

Just as quickly, one of the youths threw the entire contents of a tin of matt black paint over the windscreen while the other two slashed wildly at the tyres with bowie knives.

Steve kicked open the car door nearest to him. It clipped the heel of one of the young assailants, but didn't bring him down. The kid staggered for a few steps then sped up into a run. As quickly as they'd appeared, the attack team were gone, leaving their ruined Zephyr standing empty as its engine spluttered to a halt.

In the distance the sound of car doors slamming and a vehicle wheel spinning along the road could be heard.

Steve helped the others from the ruined motor and started to dust himself off. Kenny's car had been reduced to scrap and the Spicers were now out of sight, no doubt oblivious to the fact that they no longer had an escort. Steve spat a mouthful of warm blood onto the pavement and muttered a single word, 'McVey.'

The elephant had just fucked the lion.

***

When the Knights eventually reached the Hackney Road warehouse, it was as lifeless as a rural cemetery at midnight and just as eerie; it felt dark with something more than night, unsettling and foreboding.

From a distance everything seemed tranquil; no movement, no sound. It was only as the firm got closer that they could hear muted groaning from inside the building. Hands on tools, the firm edged slowly towards the entry. There was a small door at the side of the main shutter. Kenny jerked it open and then stood back quickly. The men's eyes strained into the murky interior, its blackness unrelieved by the distant street light; the groaning grew louder.

Steve slipped his hand inside and felt around for the light switch. The strip lights fluttered into life to reveal the only occupants – Matty and the Spicer brothers. The three men were lying flat on the cold, concrete floor, hurt and semiconscious.

It looked as if some sadistic bastard had smashed a crate and a half of whisky over them. They were covered in broken glass and soaked in blood and alcohol.

The van was nowhere to be seen.

Kenny closed the warehouse door quickly behind them as the others tried to offer comfort to the victims. They picked the broken glass off their faces and brushed it from their clothes. They were a mess, especially Adey Spicer who looked like he had just undergone some bizarre tribal scarring ceremony. There was barely a square inch of the young boxer's face that hadn't been "decorated" with cuts.

'The dirty bastards,' Kenny growled. He kicked an upturned paint can across the room, strode over to Matty, bent down and gripped him by the collar of his jacket. 'Who was it, Matty, who the fuckin' 'ell was it?'

'Whoa, take it easy, bruv,' said Steve evenly as he tried to loosen his brother's grip and calm him down.

Matty gurgled *'Pagggh...'* and then he lapsed into unconsciousness.

Kenny Knight stood up, teeth gritted. His face was a furious crimson and his lips were so compressed that the flesh around his mouth seemed to balloon out. The sharp, bright light of the warehouse emphasised the veins on the side of his head which visibly bulged and throbbed.

Steve waited for his brother to speak but he didn't. He just stood there, fists clenched, breathing deeply and angrily.

'It was Pat, wasn't it?' said Steve quietly.

Kenny's reply was a long time coming but everyone knew what answer to expect.

'Of course it fucking was.'

Bonus Short Story
WHAT YOU WISH FOR

"Oh, damn him," Jayne Titchmarsh-Harvey thought. "Damn that useless excuse for a man from here to kingdom come." Half a day she had given up – out of her very busy schedule – to go to Uncle Conrad's funeral. That's rich Uncle Conrad, who had made his millions from property development and pornography; and all the selfish old bastard had left her was *this?*

Nostrils flaring with indignation, she eyed the old-fashioned Remington typewriter with disdain.

What a useless chunk of antiquated junk.

She watched the delivery fellow deposit it on her coffee table and wait for a moment for the tip that never came. The words of Conrad's will, recited by his dim, gormless solicitor, played around her head. *"For my talented niece, may you write your next TV hit in style..."*

Jane scowled. Her next TV hit would almost certainly now involve the painful murder of a rich old porn baron suffering from halitosis and erectile dysfunction. But only as an aside of course.

All of Jayne's work – the entire Titchmarsh-Harvey oeuvre – was devoted to serial killers who preyed mercilessly on vulnerable women, usually hookers, barmaids or lap-dancers. The killers would run rings around the male detective – sexist cavemen to a man – but they would always meet their match in Elizabeth 'Lizzy' Wordsworth, Jayne's steely-eyed, tough-as-any-guy-but-feminine-with-it detective inspector.

The *Sunday Telegraph* had been queasy about the level of sadomasochistic sex and unsavoury images in her stories. Much of Jayne's blood-thirsty TV fiction bordered on autopsy-porn with lingering close-ups of horrendous injuries and maggot-infested corpses. Her victims were always debased, butchered and utterly dehumanized.

They were raped, sodomised and slaughtered in such depraved ways that had a man written the scripts, he would rightly have been accused of misogyny.

In *The Sun*, television critic Ally Ross – the industry's lone voice of sanity – observed that Titchmarsh-Harvey was "as right-on as Newt Gingrich in a peek-a-boo bra" and "a poisonous piece of work." But because Jayne's heroine was female, and all of the male characters were vile, she continued to attract the moist-gusset support of admiring feminist columnists and the vast majority of broadsheet critics. The entire liberal arts establishment sang her praises. She "provoked debate", she "confounded expectations". She was "the antidote to hegemonic masculinity". Apparently.

Her Melvyn Bragg television special was in the bag.

In just eighteen episodes over three successful prime time series, Lizzy Wordsworth had become part of the national culture. No high-ranking woman cop who was mentioned in the national press could escape being compared to her.

This year Jayne hoped that Bafta would finally reward her efforts with a gong.

"Oh isn't it lovely?" sighed her mousy PA Mandy Snell who was admiring the Remington. "I bet you can't wait to get these keys clack-clacking away. It'll be like being back in the newsroom for you."

Jayne shuddered. The one thing she never wanted to be reminded of was her time in the *Daily Star* newsroom, when she was plain Jane Watts, ashamed of her small-town Lancashire vowels, and about to have her heart broken by the news editor.

Jayne shot her PA a look she could have stored ice cream in.

"Don't insult me," she snapped. "It's junk. What possible use could I have for this?"

Mandy was stung by the sharpness of her voice.

"I'm sorry," she said, her bottom lip quivering. "I just thought that it would be nice to have something permanent to remember your uncle by. Especially as he once said he planned his career on his Remington; Conrad said he felt his soul entwined with it. I read it in…"

Her voice trailed off as Jayne's glare intensified.

"Yeah? Well let me know when your brain comes back from lunch. Have you got that new script printed out yet?"

"Not quite, still inputting it" Mandy replied, adding defensively. "I had to go into town yesterday to pick up your mourning clothes from the hire shop and…"

"Well, you've only got until Friday. Tarquin Burke-Stanley at Network Centre must have it before he leaves for Tuscany."

"I'll get on with it tomorrow."

"You do that."

"I'll…"

Jayne turned her back on her and waved her hand in the air dismissively. Mandy reddened and left the room.

Titchmarsh-Harvey wrote all of her screen-plays in long-hand. Mandy's main job, when she wasn't answering the phone, fetching papers, running errands and making coffee, was to decipher her scribbles and type them up on her PC, correcting the spelling as she went. Working here used to be fun, she reflected; but her boss had changed since the run-away success of season one. Self-important, that was the word. These days she was more full of herself than a self-catering cannibal.

Jayne poured herself a glass of Krystal champagne and sneered at the Remington. At least an antique Harrison Visible would have been worth a few bob.

So Conrad's soul was entwined with this piece of shit, was it? His arsehole more like. Idly, she slipped a sheet of A4 paper into the machine and typed one-fingered: 'Jayne Titchmarsh-Harvey wins the Lottery," she wrote. Then she laughed, tore out the paper, screwed it up and threw it in the bin.

Half a bottle and a Celine Dion CD later, she placed the typewriter in a black bin liner and carried it to the kitchen for Mandy to dispose of in the morning, giggling as she went.

It wasn't until half-way through the next morning that Jayne checked the Lotto results in the *Daily Mail*. She nearly choked on her smoked salmon bagel. The six winning numbers were all hers. The jackpot was an estimated £2.5million. There was one winner.

Her.

"Mandy!" she shrieked.

Her PA ran in to the kitchen from the office.

"Where's that typewriter?"

"I put it out in the big bins, like you wanted."

"Oh you fudge-wit!"

The woman really was as much use as a gingerbread vibrator.

Jayne shot out of the apartment in her dressing gown and slippers, a worried Mandy trotting along behind her. When they reached the bins, Jayne cupped her hands and the PA reluctantly climbed up, swinging her legs over the side to descend gingerly into the waste. It only took her a couple of minutes to fish through the filth and find the sack containing the Remington but the process had left her smelling like an unflushed Glastonbury portaloo. It would take Mandy two showers and a bath to flush away the unsavoury odours she had accumulated.

Jayne left her hapless PA dusting herself down while she rushed the machine back to the office. Putting in a sheet of A4 paper, she typed: 'Jayne Titchmarsh-Harvey wins Bafta… Jayne Titchmarsh-Harvey honoured by the Queen…' She paused, smiled and then added: 'Jayne Titchmash-Harvey meets her perfect man – six foot 2, bright, athletic, sharp-dressed toy-boy…TODAY!' Smiling to herself, she took the sheet of paper out of the typewriter, folded it up tightly and slipped it into her diary.

"Mandy," she barked. "Run me a bath!"

If she was going to meet Mr Right tonight, she was damn well going to get laid. It had been a long time.

Jayne had arranged to meet an old newspaper colleague Hillary Boisdale in a Limehouse pub – she was a frightful bore but she couldn't be seen out and about like Billy No-Mates. She should get there for six, she decided. The place was frequented by plenty of high-flying City boys.

Everything was going to plan, except that dim Mandy – she would have to go – hadn't finished inputting the script.

"It has to be at ITV by 9am tomorrow," Jayne told her PA sternly as she left. "So you jolly well stay late and get it all done. I don't care if you're here until midnight. If you don't finish, you're out of a job. Got it?"

Mandy bit her bottom lip to stop the tears.

The City Pride pub positively throbbed with testosterone. Eager to out-do each other, bullish market men flashed their cash and chatted up every "piece of skirt" in the joint...returning to boast about the women they'd "smashed up" the next day. Several tried to hit on the two women, but only one man seemed to fit Jayne's bill. Neill was six foot two with Morrissey's haircut and what looked like David Beckham's body. He was also, it transpired, five years younger than her, buff and rich enough to be wearing a brand new La Crosse XC-55 wristwatch. As soon as he clapped eyes on Jayne, he seemed transfixed by her. And this charming man proved his worth when the power cut hit. Making his excuses to Hillary, Neill swept Jayne off her feet and drove her to Booty's river-side bar, where, for a small consideration, Dennis the owner laid on candles, champagne and lasagne cooked on a camping stove – just for them.

When Neill dropped her home at 10pm, Jayne knew she had to have him. They embraced as soon as the front door was shut

— thankfully that lazy cow Mandy had already left. The sex that followed, there on the carpet, was as wild as anything Jayne had ever experienced; her orgasm was shattering in its intensity.

She fetched him a beer from the fridge – warm because of the blasted power cut. Neill listened intently and kept her brandy glass topped up as she told him about her life, her work regime and her dreams. They talked for hours. She had never met such an attentive guy.

He asked about what she would do after the Wordsworth series. She told him about her idea for a kind of super-feminist killer; a vamp who beds scores of bad men and then tortures them and kills them. "Kind of like Dexter in a skirt," he thought, but didn't say. It would be the antidote to most serial killer stories, Jayne insisted, where women are the victims. The *Guardian* would love it.

"Are you in to torture?" he asked, smiling sweetly.

"A little light play-bondage never hurt anyone," she replied coquettishly, adding "We women are all Anastasia now."

Neill scooped her up in his hands and carried her through to the bedroom where he slowly undressed her and lovingly caressed her. Then he lay her gently, face down on her double bed and tied her feet and hands to the bed-posts using his belt, his tie and the cords from her dressing gowns.

The last knot was a little too tight.

"That hurts, darling," she said.

He smacked her straight round the face, roughly pulled back her head and fastened his handkerchief around her mouth to stop her talking.

Jayne was furious. She was all for a little authenticity but really, this was too much. She started to struggle. Neill hit her again and produced a scalpel from his pocket, holding it hard against her face. Jayne froze. The anal sex that followed was nowhere near as painful as what came after; as Neill went on to violate her with a series of household objects.

The wetness she felt was her own blood.

She was on the verge of passing when he began to make the first incision by the side of her right eye. Jayne snapped wide awake. How was this happening to her?

Just as suddenly she realised.

The power cut! Obviously, Mandy hadn't been able to finish the last scenes on the computer and print it out so she would have had to have done it the old-fashioned way... on the blasted typewriter. And in the closing moments of episode one, the rich but hateful society lady was raped, beaten and then skinned alive by her latest concubine. The pitiful remains of her body would be found the next morning – or on TV in episode two – by her shocked maid, or in this case the loyal PA.

Oh Mandy, you fucking idiot.

In reality Jayne Titchmarsh-Harvey was not skinned alive and her corpse was not found until several weeks later when her neighbours reported the unpleasant stench of what they assumed were blocked drains. Mandy never came back to work. She had never finished typing out the episode either. If Jayne had bothered looking she would have found her heart-felt, hand-written resignation note on her desk, stained with her tears.

The Times was not the only newspaper to comment on the irony. Jayne Titchmarsh-Harvey, who had made her name with chilling stories about serial killers, was savagely murdered herself by a killer who preyed on wealthy middle-aged widows in a manner that bore remarkable similarities to the fiend in her second Lizzy Wordsworth series.

Neill – real name Charles Beeson – was a Wordsworth obsessive; his Stepney council flat was covered in pictures of the star, and of Jayne Titchmarsh-Harvey. His City boy life-style turned out to be as phoney as his watch, which he'd bought for 25 notes from an Albanian criminal in a pub in Shoreditch.

There was no Lizzy Wordsworth to track him down and collar Neill, of course; just a world-weary, scum-hating East

End DI who made damn sure he hurt him before slapping on the cuffs.

Jayne's obituary noted that the Bafta-winning writer, due to be made a Dame in the Queen's Birthday Honours List, had left nearly £2.75 million in the bank.

No friends or family attended her funeral; just an odd assortment of ghouls, Wordsworth fans and weirdoes. But her Melvyn Bragg television special was awash with uncritical sycophancy.

Shortly after the funeral, Mandy Snell contacted her former boss's closest relatives and asked if she could have the Remington as a keepsake to remember her old employer by and maybe write some fiction of her own. They were glad to get shot of the worthless piece of junk.

Mandy now lives in Dubai, when she isn't in her riverside pad in Chelsea; or with her two adorable sons cheering on her mega-rich footballer husband to another sensational victory at Stamford Bridge. It turned out to be a record-breaking season.

COMING in 2023:

The brand-new Face novel: **Harry Tyler in New York**.